I0553862

The White Gull

by

Laura Strickland

The Lobster Cove Series

The White Gull

Cover Art by *Diana Carlile*

The Wild Rose Press, Inc.
PO Box 708
Adams Basin, NY 14410-0708
Visit us at www.thewildrosepress.com

Publishing History
First American Rose Edition, 2015
Print ISBN 978-1-5092-0294-2
Digital ISBN 978-1-5092-0295-9

The Lobster Cove Series
Published in the United States of America

Lightning flashed once more, flooding her eyes with brightness. In the doorway of the bedroom stood a figure wearing dripping oilskins, only the matching sou'wester missing from his bare head.

Declan.

In the sudden darkness that followed the lightning, she moaned his name and then shouted it.

"Declan? Declan, Declan!"

She heard movement, the scrape of a boot on the floorboards, the flap of his coat as he turned and left the doorway.

With a sob, she followed. Hands stretched before her like a blind woman, she felt for him, stubbed her bare toe on the leg of the bedstead, and faltered. She blundered from the room in his wake.

The cottage boasted but three rooms: this bedroom they had shared, another smaller bedroom she'd dreamed of someday using as a nursery for her children, and the main room which combined parlor and kitchen. The darkness of the main room enfolded Lisbeth like black velvet. She had but a glimpse of paler darkness as the front door opened and closed again.

"Declan!"

She followed after him, her heart torn between gladness and pain. He was here! But if he truly were here, returned by some miracle from the same sea that had stolen him, why would he go from her?

She reached the door, tore it open, and stared out into the storm. Waves and salt spray poured over the stones in front of the cottage. Static filled the air, and lightning arced overhead, the thunder competing for dominance with the crash of the rain.

Praise for Laura Strickland

"The world building is phenomenal."
~Daysie W. at My Book Addiction and More
~*~

"Laura Strickland creates a world that not only draws you in, but she incorporates it…seamlessly. …the kind of book that keeps you awake well into the wee hours, and sighing with satisfaction when you've finished the very last page."

~Nicole McCaffrey, author
~*~

"As I read I became so involved with the story, I found it difficult to put down the book. …Definitely …an author to watch."

~Dandelion at Long & Short Reviews

Books by Laura Strickland
available from The Wild Rose Press, Inc.
Dead Handsome: A Buffalo Steampunk Adventure
Off Kilter: A Buffalo Steampunk Adventure
Devil Black
His Wicked Highland Ways
Daughter of Sherwood
Champion of Sherwood
Lord of Sherwood
~*~

Christmas Stories:
Mrs. Claus and the Viking Ship
The Tenth Suitor

Dedication

In memory of my ancestors,
whose hearts were anchored to the bay.
And to my editor, Nan Swanson,
for her wisdom, patience,
and the gift of her friendship.

Chapter One

Frenchman Bay, Maine, September 1851

Lisbeth O'Shea awakened from the depths of sleep abruptly, as if someone had called her name, and opened her eyes. She lay for a moment searching the intense darkness of the room with all her senses.

Outside a storm raged; she could hear wild, ragged waves clawing at the strip of shingle that fronted the cottage, and rain struck the windows intermittently as if someone threw handfuls of gravel at them.

Surely the storm had wakened her, nothing more.

She drew a breath, struggling for it, and tried to calm her racing heart. Was she alone?

Overhead the rafters creaked like the planks of an old ship. The cottage had belonged to the O'Sheas, parents of her late husband, Declan. He had grown up here, the son of a lobster fisherman. How many times had he lain in this very bed with her and teased: *Feels like I'm out in me Da's old scow when I'm rowing you in me arms, Lisbeth, darlin'.*

Lisbeth squeezed her eyes shut on a surge of grief and pain. It had been a storm like this that brought his father's old scow, the *White Gull*, ashore in pieces on the rocks down past Lobster Cove, and broke Lisbeth's heart with it. Declan had not been aboard and was nowhere to be found, plucked away clean as the jetsam

1

such storms scrubbed from the shore.

A year ago, that had been. Every time Lisbeth awoke with his voice in her ears, she told herself she had to stop hoping. But she couldn't, not quite.

Lightning flashed, sharp and violent, and seared her eyes.

Lisbeth flinched and clutched the blanket. The men of Lobster Cove—old salts and mariners, many of them—had examined the wreckage of the *White Gull* and speculated she'd been hit by lightning while at sea. No man, they said, could have ridden out such a storm.

"Not even a strong swimmer like Declan," Lisbeth said aloud, now.

The words hung in the dark air of the room, burning Lisbeth's heart the way the bright flash seared her eyes. She did not want to believe them.

She must.

Outside the wind rose, threatening a gale, and screamed around the stones of the cottage. Surely that had awakened her. Not his voice.

Lisbeth.

There—she heard it again, a mere whisper of sound riding the tail end of the thunder. Just so had his voice rumbled in her ear when he made love to her, warm and so very Irish.

Suddenly she could lie in the bed no longer. She fought her way free of the blankets and swung her bare feet down to the icy floor. Fumbling, she reached for the candle on the table beside the bed and in her haste knocked it over. She heard it roll away across the planks.

No light, then. She waited for the next flash of lightning to illuminate the tiny room. She had not wed

2

Declan for his wealth or possessions but for the charm he wore like a second skin, and the devilry in his eyes. She had married him because he was all she'd imagined wanting since the age of eleven.

She stumbled to the window and strained to see through the rain that streaked the glass. The next flash showed her the rocks in front of the cottage and the sea heaving itself up like the back of a monster to top them. The storm must be right over her. And remembering— remembering made her tremble.

She recalled the first time she'd seen Declan O'Shea. She, her sister Ellie, and her parents had just moved to Lobster Cove from St. John's, Newfoundland when Lisbeth and Ellie showed up for their first day of school at the one-room schoolhouse on First Street. Ellie, older than Lisbeth and more outgoing, took things such as the first day of school in her stride. Even before they entered the building, she struck up conversations with two girls her age and made friends.

Lisbeth, feeling shy, stood on her own, eyeing the other students—all ten of them. Some looked young enough to be just starting to learn their letters. One girl, near Lisbeth's age, wore a fine frock and button-up shoes, and stood with her nose in the air.

Three lads also appeared to be near Lisbeth's age. One stood as quietly as she, an awkward-looking boy with no meat on his bones, a pinched face, and hair black as coal. The other two had to be brothers, they looked so alike—both with flaming red hair, faces full of freckles, and eyes wild as those of foxes. The brothers fussed and pushed each other until the teacher called them all inside. Then one of them held the door for Lisbeth and gave her a smile that lit the morning—

3

and her heart. Not until the teacher called roll did Lisbeth learn his name: Declan O'Shea.

She believed she had loved him from that very day.

Another flash and again her thoughts flew back in time. It had rained on the day of their wedding—bad luck, some folks said. Lisbeth hadn't cared about the weather because Declan had become hers forevermore.

But the bad luck had followed. Almost a year to the day from her wedding had come the storm, so like this one, that had snatched Declan from her life.

She turned from the window blindly, not wanting another glimpse of the raging sea lest she begin raving at it in return, screaming and demanding what it owed her. She told herself she should bury her head under the bedclothes, burrow there, and pray for morning. How many more of these endless nights could she endure?

Lightning flashed once more, flooding her eyes with brightness. In the doorway of the bedroom stood a figure wearing dripping oilskins, only the matching sou'wester missing from his bare head.

Declan.

In the sudden darkness that followed the lightning, she moaned his name and then shouted it.

"Declan? Declan, Declan!"

She heard movement, the scrape of a boot on the floorboards, the flap of his coat as he turned and left the doorway.

With a sob, she followed. Hands stretched before her like a blind woman, she felt for him, stubbed her bare toe on the leg of the bedstead, and faltered. She blundered from the room in his wake.

The cottage boasted but three rooms: this bedroom they had shared, another smaller bedroom she'd dreamed of someday using as a nursery for her children, and the main room which combined parlor and kitchen. The darkness of the main room enfolded Lisbeth like black velvet. She had but a glimpse of paler darkness as the front door opened and closed again.

"Declan!"

She followed after him, her heart torn between gladness and pain. He was here! But if he truly were here, returned by some miracle from the same sea that had stolen him, why would he go from her?

She reached the door, tore it open, and stared out into the storm. Waves and salt spray poured over the stones in front of the cottage. Static filled the air, and lightning arced overhead, the thunder competing for dominance with the crash of the rain.

Wearing only her nightgown, Lisbeth was immediately soaked to the skin. The wind tore at her hair, and she strained to catch sight of the figure she had glimpsed in the doorway.

From the cottage, as well she knew, a path led either north to a narrow strip of shingle or south toward Lobster Cove. Which way might he have gone? She could see nothing but storm, the raging elements that matched the furor now in her heart. Would he head down to the sea? Most of this coast consisted of sheer rock, but the O'Sheas possessed that stony beach where they had hauled up their boats and readied their lobster traps.

The boats were all gone; the *White Gull* lay in pieces. Why would Declan go there? Having come home to her, why would he leave at all?

She walked barefoot to a break in the rocks where the sea poured in like a gray beast, alive and wild. No one but a madman would be down on that strip of shingle now.

She turned her head toward the track but saw nothing. The thought came to her: *Maybe I imagined it.* But she had heard the scrape of his boots on the floor. She had seen his hair ruffled by the force of the storm.

A dream, then. She'd had them before, yes, but never, never so real. She returned to the cottage, where she shut the door and hurried to the fireplace. With clumsy hands, she searched for matches and the stub of a candle. Her fingers shook so violently it took her three attempts to put flame to the wick.

The light took hold slowly and seemed pitifully inadequate. Thrusting it aloft, Lisbeth retraced her steps to the door of her room, careful to keep the hem of her now-sodden garment swept back, her eyes on the floor.

A trail of wet led its way to the bedroom door and culminated on the threshold.

The very place where he had stood.

The candle tumbled from her suddenly numb fingers, and the flame went out.

Chapter Two

The storm pulled off before dawn and moved away up the coast toward Nova Scotia. Lisbeth, who slept no more that night, dressed herself and, before going outside, mopped up the wet floor by the dim light that seeped over the windowsills.

The wind still blew aloft, raking the sky and stretching the clouds into long streamers. But areas of blue showed between, and far out the sea took on a deep cobalt hue. Inshore, the waves remained tumultuous. They tossed themselves over the break wall, sending an occasional spurt of spray half way up her walk.

She stood wrapped tight in her shawl, her hair flapping and her skirts pressed against her legs. Her gaze plundered the shore the way the storm had. She did not want to admit to herself she looked for signs— for proof—of what she had seen last night, some tangible evidence beyond the water on the floor saying she hadn't dreamed the figure in the doorway. In the hours before dawn she'd been over and over it, and doubt had crept in. She might well have dreamed it.

She must have dreamed it.

Just as she must have dropped that water on the floor herself, shed it before she caught herself, when she came in.

She must have shed it.

7

Because, desire it as she would, Declan couldn't come back to her. He lay dead somewhere at the bottom of that wild ocean.

Could the heart produce such an illusion through sheer desire?

Unable to keep still an instant longer, she walked down the path to the shingle, going carefully and marking the items that littered the stones. Such storms as the one last night swept the shore clean of flotsam and deposited new things in exchange: driftwood, broken floats, even a lobster pot lying dashed and broken.

Was it one of Declan's? After he died, the men had hauled in his pots and given her the money from his last catch. This broken cage, then, must represent someone else's misfortune.

The sea clawed at the shingle, slow to calm. Almost at once, Lisbeth's feet became soaked and cold, but she walked on. If he'd come in a skiff, he would have put in here; it was the only place.

Yet she saw no signs on the stones and, anyway, what skiff could weather such a storm?

She turned and walked the other way, back toward the path that led to town. The wind blew her hair into her eyes, and she pawed it out of the way. She had the mad idea she might find his sou'wester lying in a sodden patch of bright yellow where it had blown from his head.

Mad idea.

She passed her cottage, climbed the rise where the path angled up along the cliff toward Lobster Cove, and saw him.

A man walking toward her.

Not the man she sought.

This one had no beacon of flaming red hair declaring his Irish blood. And a dog walked at his side. The man's hair and the dog's coat matched in hue—black, with the deep gleam of a crow's wing. Lisbeth knew him by the dog and his hair, and she tried to deny the way her heart fell.

"Good morning, Rab," she called when he drew near enough. "What brings you way up here so early?"

"Came to make sure you survived that blow last night."

He and the dog kept walking toward her. A big man, and the blacksmith in town, Rab Sinclair could not be called handsome—not as Declan had been.

Handsome as the Devil, am I not? Declan had often joked, with that note of cocky confidence in his voice.

But Rabbie Sinclair had a pleasant face, broad and strong like the rest of him, and that glossy black hair worn over-long, and those deep blue eyes the same color the sea had now turned, far out. Lisbeth wondered again why he had never married; a sheer waste of a good man.

For Rabbie Sinclair was above all else a good man. Lisbeth had known him from that first day at school—the thin, dark boy straight off a ship from Scotland, orphaned and with his keep to earn in the world.

How that pale, scrawny boy had grown!

She turned her attention to the dog, a male Newfoundland. Rab had accepted him in trade three years ago for a job he'd done for some fishermen from off the Grand Banks. The dog had been a mere pup then, a ball of black fur and paws that Lisbeth had

9

helped name. Like the man, the dog had grown magnificently.

The three of them met on the path, and Lisbeth reached to pat the dog's head. "Good morning, Kelpie." She added, addressing the dog rather than his master, "Surely you did not walk all the way out here from concern for me?"

Rab shrugged his big shoulders. He wore a fisherman's sweater nearly the same color as his eyes, and Lisbeth wondered which of the townswomen had knitted it for him. Several of them pursued Rab the way they had pursued Declan before Lisbeth married him.

"Friends look out for one another," he said. The deep burr of Scotland still colored his voice after more than a decade in Maine. "Besides, Kelpie here is always eager for a walk."

Lisbeth felt his gaze touch her face in swift inspection. "Are you well, Lisbeth?"

Not wanting to lie to him outright, Lisbeth merely nodded. Rabbie, a good friend indeed, checked on her often, seeming to take the mile-long trek from Lobster Cove in stride.

She knew decency should prompt her to invite him in for a cup of tea, but the cottage stood dark and cold. Besides, she wanted to be alone to search the path for a crumpled sou'wester, for signs her dream might prove true.

The wind seized the end of her shawl and pulled it from her shoulders. Rab reached out quickly enough to keep it from soaring away.

"Mad to stand out here in the cold," he observed. "You'll catch your death."

Lisbeth looked up and encountered his gaze. The

blue eyes, trapped between black lashes, narrowed at her, and she tried to decide what she saw there: concern, surely, and the kindness Rab wore like a second skin.

He had once told her a lad cut adrift from his home at the age of fourteen—orphaned and landless, sent to a new life—learned many things quick and hard. Especially how it felt to be in need, how terrifying the world could be, and the value of kindness.

Lucky Kelpie, she thought, who had landed in his hands. And fortunate the woman who eventually won his heart.

She sighed deeply, surrendering at last the compulsion to search for what might not exist.

"Will you come in for some breakfast?"

"I will not say 'no.' "

She turned, and they walked together, back the way she had come, to the cottage. She'd left in such haste the door still stood open, driven back and forth by the wind.

What would Rab make of that? He frequently voiced the opinion that with Declan gone Lisbeth should not stay here alone.

"Any damage in town?" she asked, for something to say, as they pushed into the dim front room.

"Aye." Rabbie closed the door carefully and stood looking about. With the large dog, he seemed to overfill the room the way Declan never had.

But then, Declan was quicksilver, light and ever-moving. Rabbie was the granite of those rocks on the shore.

"That big loblolly pine—you know, the one at the head of Main Street—got hit by lightning. Came down and blocked the road."

Lisbeth, striving desperately for a natural reaction, fixed her features into an expression of shocked surprise. "Anyone hurt?"

"No one living and breathing, but plenty of property damage. Lisbeth, 'tis cold in here. Why have you let the fire go out?"

"I—" Lisbeth stared at him helplessly.

"Never mind, let me."

An expert with fire was Rab, after tending the blaze in the forge so many years. Lisbeth knew he thought it a sin to let a fire die.

Now she removed her shawl and watched as Kelpie lay down with a grunt and Rab bent over the cold hearth, his hair sliding over his forehead like black silk.

As he worked to kindle a fire, he stole little looks about the room; Lisbeth wondered what he saw. True, the place felt bleak to her, but she blamed that on Declan's absence. Her life felt bleak, withal. She supposed she had not been keeping up with things as she should. She couldn't remember the last time she'd swept the floor or shaken out the rugs. Her work lay in a pile on the wooden bench by the window—for she earned her keep as a seamstress—but little enough other color enlivened the place. It felt not only cold but uninhabited, and none of the lamps had been trimmed.

When he had the fire going to his satisfaction, Rab straightened from the hearth and looked Lisbeth in the eyes.

"Tell me, Lisbeth, when are you going to put your grief behind you and take up your life?"

Chapter Three

The interior of Lisbeth O'Shea's cottage felt like death: Rab couldn't describe it any other way. The cold that filled it went beyond the physical and struck at his soul.

He supposed that must be the fey Highlander in him talking. More than ten years out of Scotland and he had not succeeded in leaving it behind. He remembered his grandmother telling him, before his world fell apart and he was forced to leave home, "We are knowing things in our blood, lad. Never question that sense. You come by it honestly."

Rab knew now that the woman standing before him had been honed to her marrow. He would give all he had to help her, but he did not know how. He might offer friendship and comfort; he had already given her his heart.

How frail and broken she looked, stranded in this devastated place with the reflection of sorrow in her eyes! Why did he love her so completely and so helplessly? He could not say; he simply had ever since the moment he first saw her, back at the Lobster Cove schoolhouse all those years ago. Since then she had grown into a woman he could only admire— hardworking, generous and kind, giving him no reason to change his feelings.

Of course he hadn't understood what he felt for her

back then. He merely knew how much he enjoyed watching the lass who sat across the aisle and one row up from him, catching the curve of her cheek when she turned her head, counting the curls on her shoulders.

Her hair had been golden then, a child's hair still. Now it had darkened to the ashen hue belonging to a woman, but still streaked with gold from the sun. She never failed to look beautiful to him, with her delicate features and those eyes that made him think of magical things: highland mist and the color of the sea loch back home on a cloudy day.

At school she had been a comfort to him, a balm to a lad aching from the loss of everything he loved, thrown onto this rocky shore with an impossible way to make—a new master, kind but firm, and the sheer hard work of the forge. He had pinned all his dreams on Lisbeth Parsons.

She, of course, had never seen anyone but Declan O'Shea.

And the true tragedy of it, she had never once seen Declan for what he truly was.

She would not now. Declan was dead, a martyr to the sea, a memory. Lisbeth cherished him yet.

He remembered all too well the day Declan had drowned. A storm like the one just past it had been. And that had brought him out here early today, concern for Lisbeth foremost in his mind. What might the Widow O'Shea do here alone when despair overtook her?

He gazed at her now, unable to hide his concern. She'd dropped weight since Declan's death. Her fingers, which she twisted in her skirt, looked like little more than sticks.

Gently he asked, "When are you going to move into town? 'Tis not right, you out here on your own."

She shook her head and made no reply.

"There's that room at Mrs. Taylor's," he pressed. "She's still looking to let it."

"I don't want to live with Mrs. Taylor. She's a terrible gossip."

Rab knew it for truth. "But in town you'd be nearer your clients. And near your friends."

He, himself, lived in back of Howard's Blacksmith Shop on Maple Street—his now, since the death of his patron, Tip Howard, three years ago. On his deathbed Tip had told Rab he'd become more son to him than apprentice, and earned the inheritance.

"Frannie's there," he went on. Frannie Becker, Lisbeth's closest friend, was as worried about her as he.

"Frannie has two small children and her own life to live," Lisbeth replied.

"That changes nothing. Here, sit down before you fall."

Impulsively he towed her to a stool and sat her down. Then he hoisted the kettle—bone dry—and shook his head. "Have you tea in the house?"

"Some."

He snatched up a bucket for the well. Kelpie gave him a look from soulful eyes in passing.

Guard, he told the dog in his mind. The two of them did not always need words to communicate.

The wind tore at him when he went out, just like his emotions. He wanted so badly to gather Lisbeth up in his arms and carry her back to Lobster Cove—not to Mrs. Taylor's but to his quarters, warm and safe behind the shop. He longed to confess all his feelings for her, a thing he'd never done. Declan O'Shea had always stood in the way.

Rab smiled bitterly as he filled the wooden bucket. *As he did still.*

Inside, Lisbeth remained where he'd put her, which further discomfited him. For all her apparent fragility, he knew her to have a stubborn, independent streak. If that had been beaten down, she must be in even worse straits than he thought. He poured water into the kettle and swung it over the fire.

"Winter will be coming in a few months." He resumed the conversation as if it had never been interrupted. "Say you'll be away out of this place before then."

"I will think on it, Rab."

"Do you promise me?"

She nodded.

Of course, he told himself sadly, *thinking on* wasn't the same as *moving on.*

"How are you fixed for firewood?" he asked, eyeing the meager supply beside the hearth.

"I mean to gather some driftwood once the wind dies."

He turned his attention to the shelves that flanked the fireplace. "And have you enough foodstuffs? Your cupboards look unco' bare."

"I mean to go into town tomorrow and purchase a few things."

"Write me out a list; I'll bring what you want."

She stared at him. In the radiance cast by the newly-kindled fire, he saw her eyes fill with tears. "I have no money to pay, Rab. I will soon; I'm finishing a job for Mignon La Marche, and she pays well. But right now…"

"Do not worry about the coin. I will be able to get you credit at the mercantile. Have you flour? Butter? Lamp oil?"

Stonily she said, "Mr. Beatty will not give me any more credit. I have not been able to pay much on the last bill. I gave him what I could, but you see, Declan owed him quite a bit when he—"

She could not speak the word: *died*. Rab wanted to say it for her, make her face it, accept that she might resume the life she appeared to have abandoned when the damned pieces of the *White Gull* washed ashore.

But he dared not.

Very gently he told her, "I will sort it."

Kelpie, perhaps sensing Lisbeth's emotions, got up and thrust his great head onto her lap. Her hands came up and caressed the dog, buried themselves in his thick, black fur, and Rab saw her ease for the first time.

"Would you like me to leave Kelpie here with you for company?" he offered.

Again her fey, shadowed eyes flew to his. "He would be miserable away from you. You know how he likes to keep you in sight."

True, Kelpie had become a feature of the blacksmith's, always lying at the door and rarely letting Rab move far without him.

"But he loves you," Rab told Lisbeth. *I love you.* He ached to add those words.

The water in the kettle began to sing. Rab searched out two mugs and a small measure of tea, located a stub of a loaf and morsel of butter. He brewed the first, toasted the second, and presented it all to her wordlessly.

"You are far too good to me, Rab Sinclair."

He said nothing as he watched her sip from the mug and nibble at the crust without appetite. Kelpie rested his chin on her knee.

"You've not been eating," Rab observed at last, "nor looking after yourself. What would Declan say?" He delivered the last words with deliberation as he might those of a holy incantation. He himself had detested Declan O'Shea to his very roots. But if anything could make Lisbeth care, it was the thought of him.

To his surprise she laughed unsteadily. "I am not sure he would notice. Always wrapped up in his own business was Declan."

Wrapped up in himself, more like, Rab thought sourly. He had rarely met a man whose life centered more on his own needs and wants. And he did very little real business of any kind. True, he put out in the old boat he'd inherited from his father, and duly came in again, hauled a few lobster pots while he was out on the sea. But the man had been lazy to the bone, used to getting by on his charm, which he possessed in spades.

Why couldn't Lisbeth see any of that? She never had, though, and regarded her husband still as some kind of minor Irish god.

Lisbeth had worked as a seamstress even while Declan lived, helping to keep the household. She had done what she could to maintain the cottage, just like Declan's mother before her. The O'Shea men of this shore, father and sons alike, had been feckless.

Both Declan's parents had predeceased him, his mother from overwork and his father in a drunken fall. His brother Pat had left Lobster Cove right after the pieces of the *White Gull* washed ashore. He hadn't been out with Declan that fateful day, too smart to take the boat to sea with a blow coming, and had been safe in the tavern with friends.

"He would not want you pining away here, still," Rab told Lisbeth, not sure but it was a lie. Who knew what had motivated Declan besides his own welfare? He had loved holding people in thrall to him, especially women. Indeed, before these two wed he'd been chased by many a lass, including the Mignon Lisbeth had just mentioned, who now owned the big house up on the bluff.

Mignon—also used to getting what she wanted—had chased Declan mercilessly. Rab had prayed Declan would choose her, but in the end he had chosen this pale slip of a lass with the wide eyes, spill of fair hair, and—back then—merry laugh.

That didn't mean he had been faithful to her.

Rab closed his eyes for a moment, fighting the desire to tell Lisbeth all he knew, destroy this vision she cherished of her dead husband, free her from the past to—he hoped—love again. He couldn't. He feared it would destroy not only Lisbeth's opinion of her husband but her spirit.

"Come back to town wi' me," he beseeched, speaking from his heart. "Do not make me leave you here alone."

"That's just it." She set her mug aside, leaned forward, and touched Rab's hand. He felt the imprint of her fingers all the way up his arm, to his heart. "I am not alone," she confided, "for I saw Declan last night."

Chapter Four

"I am worried about Lisbeth," Rab announced. He stood in the doorway of Frannie Becker's kitchen, feeling far too large for the cramped space. Mad confusion reigned: Frannie had two bairns under the age of two, the newest a babe of barely six months, now held in her arms. The toddler, a robust lad, ran rather than walked everywhere and seemed particularly vocal with his demands.

Frannie shot Rab a look. "Close the door for pity's sake, before Eddie escapes again. I've no desire to chase him down the street another time."

Rab eased the door shut behind his considerable bulk, trying to occupy as little space as possible. "You have your hands full there, and no mistake," he observed. Maybe Lisbeth was right; Frannie had no room and likely little energy to spare. "Where's Ed?"

"At work. He went in early; we need the coin."

Ed Becker worked at Sawyer's lumber yard all the hours God sent, to keep his little family.

Frannie shifted the bairn—a daughter—in her arms. "I'm worried about Lisbeth as well, Rab. She's stopped coming to church. And she used to walk in sometimes to see me. The Lord knows I was in no condition to walk out there when I was carrying this little one." She jostled the child. "Worse than that, she seems to have lost her spark and that strength she

20

always had about her, beneath all the softness. I'd go see her, but…"

"Aye, I see."

Wee Eddie began climbing the back of a chair, which wobbled beneath him. Rab snatched the lad up in his arms. Eddie, sticky all over his face with what looked like jam, smiled at him.

"I also see this fellow's had his breakfast."

"Would you like a cup of tea?"

"Just had one." He thought of the gloomy cottage he'd left, and the woman in it. "I walked out to see Lisbeth this morning."

"How did she come through the storm?"

Rab shook his head. "I saw no damage. But you're right, Frannie. She's not the lass she was, nor right in herself, in her mind."

"In her mind?" Frannie echoed. She stared at Rab, her eyes the same exact size and shape as Eddie's—deep brown. "I know she's still in mourning—it's only been a year—but though it's taken the heart out of her I did not think it had turned her mind." Frannie lowered her voice. "You know how she loved him."

"Aye." Rab felt sick inside. Frannie, no fool, had a good idea what Declan's true character had been. But Rab had managed to hide from her his true feelings about Lisbeth.

He drew a deep breath and set Eddie down carefully. "She says she saw him—*Declan*—last night."

"What!" Frannie's mouth fell open, and for an instant Rab thought she'd drop the child in her arms. He could see her thoughts move in her wide eyes. "Well, she must have dreamed it. That storm will have brought things back."

"That's what I thought. But she was insistent. Says there was water all over the floor where he stood in the doorway of their room."

"Sweet mercy! Did you see the water?"

"She had already mopped it up."

"It will be her imagination, poor lamb."

"Aye, but I tell you it went hard with me, leaving her out there alone, Fran. She's not looking after herself—almost no food on her shelves, and the place was cold. I collected some driftwood before I came away, and I mean to take her a load of things from Beatty's."

"You're a good friend, Rab Sinclair."

"Not good enough, letting her get in that state."

"What can I do to help?"

"I was hoping you'd persuade her to move into Lobster Cove. I did my best to convince her; she would no' listen."

"I'd go and talk to her, gladly, but—" Frannie gestured helplessly, encompassing the room and the children. "I'll try and make it out there in the next few days—I can ask Ed's mother to look after these two for a few hours. I'll take Lisbeth one of my seed cakes. She used to love them."

"I would appreciate it. She may listen to you better than me."

"I hope so."

"I offered to leave Kelpie there with her, the place seemed so lonely. She would no' hear of it."

"A shame she and Declan never had a child, something of him she might keep." Fran sighed. "Anyway, you'd make a strange sight without Kelpie at your side. Where is he now?"

"Just outside the door," Rab admitted. "Frannie, when you go to visit, try and persuade her away out of that place for the winter."

"I promise to do my best. Now you had better get off. You've a forge to run."

"Aye, and half a dozen jobs waiting."

Yet he hesitated. "You do no' suppose grief truly has unsettled her mind?"

Frannie looked concerned. "If it has you this worried, I'll go out and see her tomorrow. I'll let you know what I think then."

"Aye," he murmured, but he went away little comforted.

****

Beating on glowing iron and sweating over the forge usually brought Rab a measure of peace, but not today. Stripped down to his trousers, protected by only a leather apron, he enjoyed exercising muscles built over time and using skill combined with intention to accomplish a job. Hot iron might be mutable; fire was not. A living substance, it required accommodation, tending, and consideration if it were to cooperate with him. Over the past years at work in this place, he and fire had come to terms. He respected it and it consented to do his bidding—most of the time.

Tip Howard, who had liked to talk while he worked and especially liked to talk to the young Scots lad who remained mostly silent, used to say that in ancient times blacksmiths were considered wizards, wreakers of magic. They controlled the fire and caused iron to obey them. Not many men could survive the forge, a truth Rab learned in the most personal way as he grew. It took a certain kind of man.

"Either the fire chooses you or it doesn't," Tip told him at the beginning. "Let's see, lad, if it will heed you."

It had, but persuading it required an enormous amount of work, sweat, and more singed skin than Rab could measure. He knew, now, the fire took its price.

As did the sea, he supposed.

In the old days, the magician smiths had wrought swords and other weapons that, if strong enough, brought victory in battle. Now Rab made plows and other farm implements, horse shoes, and fancy fenders for women's hearths.

He tossed the black hair out of his eyes and wiped his perspiring forehead with an equally sweaty forearm. Today the work brought him very little contentment. He couldn't keep his thoughts from the cottage up the shore.

Aye, well, he would finish up a few jobs, go to Beatty's, and see could he run some things back out there before the light died.

He pumped up the fire and began making a list in his mind: she would need flour, lard, eggs, some dried peas, and butter if he could get it. Vegetables would be fine if Beatty had any—carrots and potatoes. And he should take something to tempt Lisbeth's appetite, just in case Frannie did not make it out there with the seed cake. But what?

Upon the thought, he heard Kelpie's tail thump. The dog lay just outside the door in the pale sunshine; a wag was his usual greeting to visitors.

Rab looked up and saw a woman enter. Women usually sent their men to the forge; this woman, though, had never married.

The teacher at the schoolhouse, Emily Cooper must be a year or two older than Rab. Plain to look at, she had a lively, intelligent mind and a droll sense of humor Rab enjoyed. Lately she had made any excuse possible to come to the shop, bringing broken implements for the school and her home. He had just completed the latest, a handle for the classroom woodstove.

"Never say it has grown so late," he greeted her. "School over already?"

"I just dismissed the children."

Ah, and he would need to get to Beatty's and up the shore before it got much later.

"I have your handle all ready." He swung away, picked up the piece from the bench, and turned back to catch Miss Cooper staring at his nether regions.

Not used to women looking at him that way, he felt a stab of surprise at the speculation in her eyes.

Miss Cooper, apparently not a bit discomfited, smiled at him. "I can always rely on you, Mr. Sinclair, to take care of my little projects." She swung her purse up by its strings. "What do I owe you?"

"Only our agreed price."

She came closer, and he considered her; tall and slender, she wore her soft, brown hair in a loose bun at the nape of her neck. She might be a fine woman, but she was no Lisbeth.

She placed the coin in his palm, being sure to let her fingers linger. "Thank you. You do such fine work. I keep saying I should bring the children down here one nice afternoon, let the lads see a man's work."

Rab mopped his forehead again, but not from the heat this time. "That's an interesting idea."

"Will you be taking an apprentice?"

"I hadn't thought on it." He'd hoped for a son of his own, but that did not look likely in the near future.

"I have a student—Dougie Grier. You know him?"

"Sure."

"Born on the wrong side of the blanket, you understand. Just like his younger brother."

Rab blinked. Most woman of his acquaintance didn't speak of such things. Dougie's mother, Maggie, worked selling ale at the Hogshead and occasionally, so it was rumored, sold or gave away her favors, as well. He'd heard her sons had two different fathers.

"Dougie's a good lad," Miss Cooper went on, "big for his age. He struggles with his letters and numbers, but he listens and tries hard. I think he'd do better with his hands than his head."

"This job takes both." Rab shrugged. "But send him round. Not today—I have an errand to run."

"I will. You're a good man, Rab Sinclair."

"I was given a chance at his age." And he'd always been grateful. "Why can't I offer the same?"

"His mother's no better than she should be, but at least she's sent him to school. And we can't hold her behavior against him."

"Certainly not. If I do decide to take him on, I would want him to keep attending school, as well." That was something upon which Tip had insisted, for him.

"Just because you earn your living by your brawn doesn't mean you have to be an ignoramus, lad," he'd said in his understated Yankee way. "Get your letters and your sums, so you'll know when a man's trying to cheat you. Learn to read books, and you'll never pass a lonely night."

26

That last was a lie: Rab had spent a boatload of lonely nights with a book in his hands.

Miss Cooper nodded as if satisfied and turned away to the door. At the last minute she looked back. "Will you be attending the autumn dance, Mr. Sinclair?"

He made a rueful gesture. "Can you see me dancing?"

"As a matter of fact, I can." To his increased shock, she winked at him before she went out the door and left him staring.

Chapter Five

Lisbeth heard the rattle of the pony trap before it came in sight and knew who approached without looking. Only one person in Lobster Cove brought a pony along the coast road; for most folks, travel by foot proved good enough.

She gathered up the gown on which she'd been stitching and hurried to peer out the door. As expected, she saw Mignon La Marche's cart come into view and halt at the rise. Even Mignon would have to walk from there.

And what had brought the fine widow La Marche all the way out from Lobster Cove? Granted it was a pleasant day, all sunlight dancing off a sea gone calm and fluffy clouds sailing the blue sky. Yet even that should not bestir Mignon from the comfort of her mansion.

Lisbeth smoothed her hands down her crumpled apron and straightened her spine. Mignon invariably made her feel inadequate—always had, even when they were at school together. Mignon, daughter of the man who had once owned the lumberyard, wore an air of privilege like she wore her stylish gowns, ordered straight from London. Mignon had put her hair up before any of the other girls, wore fine stockings and button-up shoes, and real topaz stones at her ears.

No surprise that when Claude La Marche, a

shipping baron who had made his fortune in Boston, moved to Lobster Cove and built the big house on the bluff, Mignon accepted his proposal of marriage even though he was thrice her age. That had been right after Lisbeth and Declan wed, as a matter of fact. Right up till then, Mignon had chased Declan with all her intent.

He'd chosen Lisbeth in the end, the only time Lisbeth had ever won out over her rival. But Mignon had done well for herself, netting a wealthy husband who passed away not six months later, leaving her his fortune.

And Mignon did not seem to harbor any ill feelings toward Lisbeth. She always behaved pleasantly when they met and went out of her way to give Lisbeth her sewing trade.

She came down the path now moving like a queen, her auburn hair shining in the sun. She wore it coiffed in braids that coiled around her head, and when she drew near enough Lisbeth saw that the stones in her ears today were diamonds.

"Good afternoon, Lisbeth," she called.

"Good afternoon."

"I have come to see about my gown. I thought I might need a second fitting."

Lisbeth pictured the shabby, barren room behind her and hesitated to ask Mignon in. But she could hardly be rude when the woman offered her custom. Anyway, they were friends of a sort, weren't they? Or at the very least, close acquaintances.

"It is very nearly finished. I intended to bring it to town when it was done."

Mignon paused on the path and gave Lisbeth a lively look from eyes nearly the same color as her hair.

"You do know I need it by Saturday. That's the dance."

"Yes, of course."

Mignon tipped up her chin and asked with a hint of challenge, "Are you going to ask me in?"

Wordlessly, Lisbeth stepped aside. Mignon swept by, trailing scent that matched her name.

"Ah, you have been working on it," Mignon said, catching sight of the pile of fabric Lisbeth had just laid aside on the bench in the good light. "Let me see."

Lisbeth hastened to catch up the gown and hold it for display. Peacock blue, the fabric must have cost enough to feed Lisbeth for a year. She'd taken pleasure in just touching it while she cut and sewed. The gown seemed an indecent extravagance for a town dance, but who was she to judge?

"I've only to finish the hem," she said. "There's a great deal of it." Yards and yards of the gorgeous brocade had gone into the skirt, and Lisbeth's tiny stitches did not progress quickly.

"Hmm," Mignon said. "I am not sure I like the color after all."

"Really? I think it's wonderful."

"Do you?" Mignon tipped her head. "But then, it would look better on you than me. Is it really my shade?"

"I should think this would look splendid on anyone."

"Never mind. I will try it on, and you can make sure it needs no further alteration. I want it tight, remember, across here." She indicated her generous bosom. "Shall I go into your bedroom?"

Lisbeth's heart rebelled; she did not want Mignon in her room where she had lain with Declan. "Use the spare room." She walked to the door of it. "Neater."

Mignon went in but left the door open. She called out, "What reason do you have to be less than neat? No one to mess up the place—you're just like me, a woman living alone. I rattle around in that big house until sometimes I think I will go mad."

"Will you have a cup of tea and a biscuit?" Lisbeth asked, suddenly grateful Rab had stopped back out last night with the promised groceries. If Mignon paid her today, she could repay him. But Mignon would likely not pay till the dress was completed.

"I think we have a problem," Mignon called. "The waist is too tight."

She appeared in the doorway wearing the gown, and Lisbeth was impressed by her own skill. The gown looked stunning, the color bright against Mignon's pale skin, the bodice tight, low, and daring.

"I cannot button it," Mignon admitted ruefully.

"Truly? But I measured most carefully."

"No doubt my fault rather than yours, Lisbeth. I have been comforting myself in my loneliness with crème cakes and puddings."

She turned about. Lisbeth saw a gap of nearly an inch where the back of the gown refused to meet.

"Can you fix it?"

"I can let out the side seams."

"By Saturday? I have my heart set on wearing it, despite the color."

"I am sure I can get it done."

"You are such a diligent soul—always were, even back in school." Mignon let the gown drop and stood unashamed in her chemise, which was embroidered all over and far finer than anything Lisbeth had ever owned.

"Will you be going to the dance?" Mignon asked as she stepped from the skirt.

"I don't think so."

"Never mean to say you're still in mourning! It's been over a year, hasn't it?"

"Yes."

"We widows must stick together. Say you'll attend with me."

Should Lisbeth admit she had nothing to wear? She didn't want to go anyway. So she merely shook her head and gathered the gown up from the floor.

"You know," Mignon said, "that truly would look so much better on you than me. Tell you what—why don't I give it to you after the dance, in payment? You can alter it to fit."

Lisbeth's cheeks flamed. "That's a kind thought..."

"It's worth more than I promised to pay you, you know."

"I do not doubt it. But the truth is," Lisbeth swallowed her anger and humiliation at having to admit it, "I need the money instead. I owe quite a bit at Beatty's, and to Rab Sinclair, as well."

Mignon immediately looked stricken. "I should have thought. Payment in full it shall be, and perhaps a bit extra, eh, for the work to which my waistline is putting you?"

"I would appreciate that." Suddenly, Lisbeth felt very like a servant standing before her mistress. The feeling further heated her cheeks.

"You know, I'm pleased with that," Mignon said thoughtfully. "I've never before trusted you with an entire gown, have I? Just mending and alterations. But

I'm impressed. You have some talent. Just as well." Something gleamed in Mignon's eyes, a flash too swift for Lisbeth to identify. "Since you now need to make your own way in the world."

Lisbeth had worked, and hard, while Declan was alive. But she said, "I'm grateful for all the business you send my way."

"Of course."

"Why don't you get dressed, and I'll make the tea."

"I really shouldn't stay. I have a man coming out from Augusta to fit new carpets."

Mignon disappeared back into the spare bedroom. Lisbeth stood wishing she might ask for an advance on the gown so she could put something down at Beatty's. Then she wouldn't need to rely on Rabbie's generosity to eat.

How had Declan managed to run up such a steep bill at Beatty's, anyway? She had always given him a little money from her sewing to put down on their account. Things never should have got so out of hand.

Mignon emerged from the spare bedroom dressed in her stylish walking suit, setting her hat on her head.

"Say you'll come to the dance with me," she urged again. "You can't carry the torch for Declan forever. Surely you want to marry again?"

Lisbeth blanched at the very thought. "Do you?"

"Of course. Not that I expect to find anyone suitable. Pickings are lean in this God-forsaken place."

"Why don't you move away, if you're not happy here? You have the money."

"I've thought about it—thought about Boston or even Montreal. But I can't say I'm not happy here. And who knows?" One side of Mignon's mouth curled up in a wry smile. "A man—the perfect man—could turn up at any time, one with flaming red hair, perhaps, and tawny eyes."

Lisbeth gasped; Mignon had just described Declan.

Chapter Six

"Rab sent you, didn't he?" Lisbeth looked her best friend, Frannie Becker, full in the eyes. "Do not lie to me."

Frannie squirmed and shifted in her chair at the table upon which she had proudly set the seed cake she'd baked. "Why should I need Rab to send me? I'm finally smaller than a woodshed and only too glad to leave the children with Ed's mother for a walk up the shore."

"How is little Bess?"

"Fussy, but not near the handful Eddie was—still is, truth be known. I told Ed if he comes near me again before a year has passed, I shall level him with an oar. Still, they're a blessing."

She sighed and, not giving Lisbeth a chance to reply, chatted on. "A shame you and Declan never had a child—part of him for you to keep, like." Immediately the words were out she looked stricken. "Oh, I am sorry—I did not mean to remind you."

"Do you think I need reminding?" Lisbeth had wanted Declan's child and couldn't imagine why she had not conceived. Not for lack of trying on Declan's part. "Hard to raise a child without its father, anyway."

"That's true. Perhaps it wasn't God's will for you to have a child. The good Lord must have known you'd be widowed so soon." Wildly, Frannie cast about for something else to say. Her gaze fell on the pile of blue fabric on the bench. "Do you have a commission? Who's it for?"

"Mignon La Marche."

"Oh, her." Frannie sniffed. "Remember what a trial she used to be to us in school? Always acting better and wealthier than the rest of us and tattling when we did something wrong. And oh, how she set herself at Declan!"

"Now she truly is far wealthier than the rest of us." Lisbeth gazed away through the front door, which stood open, for a glimpse of the sea. How pretty and innocent it looked today—not like an enemy that would steal a woman's husband.

"Wealthier, that's all!" Frannie protested. "The money and that fine house don't make her better than everyone."

"She tried to give me that dress, once it's a hand-me-down, in payment." Lisbeth's voice hardened with indignation. "As if I'd have any use for it."

"Not surprising. She always did act like the queen of Lobster Cove, and treated the rest of us like servants. I confess I cannot abide the woman."

"I need her custom," Lisbeth said baldly. She focused on her friend. "Are you sure Rab didn't send you to try and persuade me to move to town?"

Frannie looked uncomfortable. "He might have mentioned he thought it a good idea. You have to admit, Lisbeth, it would make things easier. Do you really want to spend another winter out here? And it would be lovely having you near."

"I can't just up and leave, though, Fran."

"Why not? Is it because of Declan, because his

memory's here, I mean?"

Lisbeth's gaze sharpened. "Just exactly what did Rab tell you?"

Frannie pushed the seed cake aside and leaned across the table, her brown eyes full of compassion. "He told me you think you saw Declan."

"I confided that to him, not to be bandied about."

"And he told no one but me. He's worried about you, Lisbeth, out here on your own, having wild fancies. Now I'm worried, too."

"I'm not sure it was a wild fancy. He stood right there in the doorway of the bedroom, Frannie, in his oilskins."

"It had to be a dream, though, didn't it, dear? Had you been asleep?"

"Yes, but something woke me—the storm—"

"You thought you woke; plainly you didn't. You dreamt it, Lisbeth, a dream of longing. Because he's gone, isn't he?"

"Is he?" Lisbeth challenged. "His body was never found."

"Many fishermen who die at sea are never found. The pieces of the boat came ashore; how could he survive in such a storm if his boat broke up?"

"He spoke my name. I heard his boots scrape on the floor."

"You know how real some dreams can be." Frannie drew a breath. "I think Rab's right; you need to get away from here."

Lisbeth tangled her fingers together on the surface of the table. "What if he comes back here looking for me and I've gone? How will he know where to find me?"

Frannie's eyes filled with ready tears. "Love, he's not coming back. And you need to get on with your life. It's been a year—time enough for your heart to heal."

"Is it? Who says so?"

"Listen, why don't you look for a room in town, just for the winter? Come spring, you can always come back here and open this place up. That's a fair compromise, isn't it?"

"I promised Rab I'd think about it, and I will. I'm grateful to both of you for your concern, truly I am. I just wish you believed me when I tell you what I saw."

"I believe what you think you saw—and that you want to believe it. I think that's what worries me most. When will Mignon's gown be done?"

"She needs it for the dance this Saturday."

"When you take it to her, stop by and see me. We'll talk again. Meanwhile, I'll leave the seed cake. Promise you'll eat some."

"I will, with the greatest delight."

"Then I'd best go before Ed's ma tears her hair out." Frannie rose from the table, glanced about, and shivered. "There's just something about this place, even on a sunny day. Can't you feel it?"

Lisbeth could.

****

The bright sunshine did not last. Well before sundown, clouds began to gather over the sea, and the wind freshened. Lisbeth smelled the rain.

She wrapped her shawl about her shoulders and went to walk the shingle, staring out into the water and beseeching all the gods who held it in their sway, "If he lives—if you have not stolen him—return him to me."

She paced until it grew too dark to see and the

38

clouds closed in. Rain began to fall, cold and sharp, as she went inside and lit the lamps, blessing Rab under her breath for the oil he'd brought. She didn't know how she would ever be able to repay his kindness.

The cottage, like the clouds, seemed to close down around her, stifling. She changed into her nightclothes and sat by the fire, listening to the rain strike the windows, unwilling to go to bed.

Not wishing to waste the precious lamp oil, she at last blew out all the lights but one that she left burning deep into the night. She must have dozed beside the fire, for the sound of the latch lifting roused her from sleep.

She raised her head just as the door swung open. Rain entered first, shedding onto the floor and preceding the figure of a man.

Lisbeth's heart leaped sickeningly in her chest. She came out of her seat as if hauled up by strings.

"Declan."

Once more his head lay bare, the flame-red hair drenched and dark from the rain, or as if he had just come out of the deep. Raindrops ran down his cheeks like tears, and his tawny eyes looked wide and vacant as if he did not know her.

"Declan!"

He halted as if she'd struck him. His body jerked like that of a man coming out of a dream. He whirled and went out the door, back into the darkness.

"Declan! Wait!"

Without a thought, Lisbeth followed him, leaving the door ajar. Outside, the wind seized her and dashed rain into her eyes. She strained for sight of him and caught just a glimpse of the yellow oilskins on the path that led toward town. Heedless, she followed, still calling his name, head and shoulders bare and with nothing but house slippers on her feet. She ran up the slope in Declan's wake, where the wind buffeted her more strongly. It tore her hair loose and streamed it across her eyes. When she could see once more, Declan had disappeared from view.

"Come back!" she screamed. "Come back to me!"

When he did not answer, she ran on into the darkness.

Chapter Seven

Rab eyed the lad who stood before him: shoulder high, thin as a string bean, and trying hard not to show his trepidation. Emily Cooper had sent her student, Dougie Grier, by after school, and Rab had just finished showing him the forge, during which the boy had not uttered a word.

He remembered himself when Tip Howard had taken him on—every bit as thin as this lad, not as tall, and twice as frightened. Tip had been firm and kind; one of the best things he'd done for Rab was feed him.

Dougie Grier appeared a mongrel, for sure, with a dusky hue to his skin and dark, careful eyes. He didn't look like he'd been sired by anyone from Lobster Cove, and Rab wondered where his mother had come by him.

"Well, what do you think?" he asked. "Do you suppose you'd like to work here?"

Dougie wetted his lips and cast his eyes about doubtfully. "Looks like hard work—sir." He added the last word as an afterthought. Not a bad thing.

"It is hard work: man's work. But that's what you'll want to be, isn't it—a man?"

Dougie nodded.

"Mind, if you apprentice with me, you'll be the dogsbody. All the dirty jobs at first, that's how I started out. That's how you learn. But if you apply yourself, you'll have a trade you can use anywhere to make a

41

living."

"Yes, sir." The respect came easier this time. Dougie brightened. "I like your dog. I wouldn't mind looking after him."

Kelpie liked the lad too—a good sign.

Rab made up his mind. "What do you say we give it a trial, say, three weeks? You come every day after school and on Saturdays. Sundays, no doubt, your ma will want you to go to church."

Dougie gave him an incredulous stare. "Never been in church, me."

"No? Well, we'll give it the three weeks. If you hate it, you quit; no hard feelings and I won't waste my time with you. If I don't think you're going to work out, same thing."

"All right, Mr. Sinclair."

"This is all with your ma's permission, mind."

Dougie's face fell. "I don't know as she'll care."

"All the same, I'll just walk you home now, shall I, and ask her." Rab put his hand on the lad's bony shoulder. "Come along."

Dougie's mother lived in a tiny house out back of the Hogshead Tavern. Rab wondered if the stories about Maggie Grier were true, and if so whether she ever took her clients to the house when Dougie was there.

She opened the door to Rab's knock clad in nothing more than a chemise and a robe which hung open in the front, and eyed Rab up and down.

"I know you: the blacksmith." She jerked her head at Dougie. "What's he done?"

"Nothing wrong." Rab launched into an account of his intentions, explained how Dougie's teacher had pointed the boy in his direction and that he was willing to try training him.

Maggie's eyes narrowed. "You want to 'prentice him?"

"Aye, if he works hard."

"What's in it for me? Do you pay him?"

"No, ma'am, I can't afford to pay him. He'll get his training and fed when he's with me."

"Ma?" Dougie tugged at her arm. "Ma, I want to."

"Well—I still think there should be something in it for me."

"There's something in it for *him*, ma'am. He'll be able to earn a steady living someday, maybe help you out."

"'Bout time he paid me back for all the food he's shoved down his piehole. I'd need him home in the evening, mind, when I take my shift. He has to watch his brother."

As if at a signal, a baby began to wail somewhere in the house.

"Just a minute," Maggie said and went off in response, leaving Rab at the door.

Dougie looked at Rab uneasily. Before he could speak, Maggie came back with a squalling infant. "I can't talk now," she said. "This one wants to eat. You can take Dougie after school and make sure you give him supper before you send him home."

Rab did not reply, being far too busy staring at the infant in her arms, who sported a crop of flaming red hair and stared back at him with Declan O'Shea's tawny eyes.

****

"Mr. Sinclair! Mr. Sinclair!"

No sooner had Rab returned to the shop, still half stunned by what he had seen and struggling to find a ready excuse for it, than a lad came in calling his name. Rab recognized him as Frannie's neighbor.

Breathless, the boy paused in the doorway of the shop and said, "Mrs. Becker sent me. She says come quick to Doc Stevens'. A friend of yours is there."

Rab's heart dropped to his toes. "A friend? Did she give a name?"

The lad shook his head. "She only said to come."

Rab ran with Kelpie at his heels and soon left the neighbor lad behind. Doc Stevens kept his surgery down the other side of Main Street, and folks stared as Rab and the big dog jogged by. Last night's rain had cleared, but the afternoon remained gloomy with cloud, as if threatening to let loose again any time, and the air held a chill.

Frannie met him at the outer door of Doc Stevens' surgery, her face pale and her soft, brown eyes full of worry.

He spoke but one word. "Lisbeth?"

Frannie nodded. "She was found lying up on the path that leads down from her cottage, senseless and soaked to the skin."

"When?"

"Brought in less than an hour ago. Fortunately, she was spotted from the water by a couple of lobstermen. It took a while to collect her and get her here to town."

Rab cursed under his breath as Frannie led him into the waiting room, using words he did not usually employ. The waiting room stood empty; it must not be regular hours for the doctor.

"She hurt?" he asked shortly.

"Wet, as I say, and very cold. She wore only her nightclothes, and her slippers were in shreds. Thing is, Doc is having trouble rousing her."

"In her nightclothes?" Rab repeated. "Never say she was lying there since last night!"

"I fear so. Nobody much uses that path. There's a small bump on her temple. Doc thinks she may have hit her head when she fell."

The surgery door opened, and Doc Stevens appeared. A man in his forties and a typically crusty New Englander, he had a long face like a horse and shrewd, blue eyes.

"Come on in," he bade them.

Bidding Kelpie to wait, Rab followed the doctor, who led them through an examining room to another small room beyond. This had been furnished with a cot, and in the bed lay Lisbeth, looking small as a child.

Rab's heart quivered in his chest and fell again, sickeningly.

"Mrs. Becker tells me you're a good friend to Mrs. O'Shea," Doc Stevens said.

"Aye, since childhood."

"I did not like to leave her alone," Frannie said, "but I must get back home. I left the children with a neighbor and have to collect them."

"I'll stay," Rab said hoarsely, his gaze touching Lisbeth everywhere, and Frannie went out.

Doc Stevens cleared his throat. "She has a bump on her forehead, as you can see, but that's no reason for her to remain unconscious so long. She was dangerously chilled when brought in, but my main concern is in rousing her."

"How long do you think she lay up there on the

path?"

"Must have been a good time, judging from her attire when found, and the rain never let up till midmorning." Doc Stevens shook his head. "I've got her out of the wet clothing and warmed her. Now she needs to wake and tell us what happened." He slanted a look at Rab. "I understand she lives on her own up the shore."

"Ever since her husband died—Declan O'Shea, who drowned last year."

"Hmm." Doc Stevens made an indeterminate sound; Rab wondered what it meant. Did the good doctor have an opinion about Declan O'Shea?

Still haunted by what he had seen at Maggie Grier's house—Declan's distinctive hair and eyes on an illegitimate bairn—Rab could only shake his head. Doctors knew things—often things they were unable to divulge.

"Sit with her and see can you rouse her," the doctor told him. "She may respond to your voice. I'll be through here in the surgery. Call me if she wakes."

Rab nodded and sank into the chair beside the cot even as the doctor went out.

"Ah, bonny lass," he murmured. He reached out one big hand and caressed her head where a livid bruise stood out, let his fingers slide very gently down her cheek. "Lisbeth, angel, list to me."

Her eyelids, thin and pale as paper, stirred but did not open. Throat tight, he took her hand in both of his in an effort to warm it—to warm her.

He feared he knew what had taken her down the shore in the night: she would have thought she saw Declan again, and probably tried to follow him. Rab cursed once more under his breath. Damn the man anyway. He had never deserved her love.

And now Rab might have stumbled on proof of that, might he not? He had long suspected Declan O'Shea of unfaithfulness. Rumors about him had run rife both before he wed Lisbeth and after, when tales were whispered about him being in the ale house when he should be out hauling pots. *The ale house where Maggie Grier worked.*

Talk was just talk, as Rab well knew. But Maggie's bairn might well be evidence. If Lisbeth saw the child, would she then accept the fact that the man she idolized might not have been all she believed? Might that be enough to free her from the spell under which Declan held her yet?

Rab contemplated his motives as he chafed her fingers very gently. Aye, he wanted to free her—but why? Was it for her sake, to open her eyes at last so her heart could begin to heal and she would stop chasing will-o-the-wisps? Or was it for his, in the hope she might choose to marry again?

Chapter Eight

"Declan!"

In her dream, Lisbeth still followed her husband through the wind and the rain. A glimpse of his yellow slicker, which had disappeared into the darkness, reappeared again ahead, just beyond a cluster of rocks. Breathless now and aching, she ran on, her slippers in shreds.

"Declan, wait for me!"

Miraculously, he did. When she reached the rocks he stood there, his head bare to the elements and his eyes still holding that wide, vacant expression.

"Declan, oh, thank God you're alive!"

She reached for him, caught his hands, and they felt colder than hers. He might be dead for all the warmth of him. His eyes stared like those of a dead man.

"Declan, do you know me?"

"Lisbeth."

Her name came in a gurgle as it had that first night when he spoke it at the door of her room.

"What's happened to you? Where have you been?"

"Dead. I am to say I was dead."

"But that's not so." She jostled his hands. "You're here with me now."

"Belong to another now."

"Another? Who?"

He tore his hand from her grip and gestured wildly at the sea. "My mistress. She has claimed me for all time."

"But we were married before God—"

"No. No, Lisbeth, no more. Go about your life. 'Tis what I came to tell you. Go about your life."

Pain blossomed in Lisbeth's head as the stony path came up to meet her. She found her face pressed against the ground while the rain beat at her. She wanted to move, longed to raise her head and see whether Declan had gone, but she could not.

She heard no step on the ground, no sound other than the hard patter of the rain, the crash of the waves below, and the wind rushing over all. But her heart told her he had gone.

Or maybe not. A soft touch skimmed her temple and her cheek, the merest brush of fingers that trailed warmth. But no, that couldn't be Declan; Declan had never touched her that way. With beguiling charm, yes, with confident seduction, and on occasion with demand. But never with this pure tenderness.

She could feel love emanating from whoever sat beside her, pure and strong. The warmth of it flowed into her and penetrated to her very bones. *To her heart.*

And that foolish organ, battered from straining after Declan O'Shea, stirred and tried to rise like a bird on the wing.

She opened her eyes. Rabbie Sinclair's face hung above her, his forehead marked with lines she had never seen there before, placed by worry. They made him look older, and that gave her a shock. Why had she never noticed he was no longer the skinny black-haired lad who had hesitated to speak for his thick, highland

49

accent? They were, all of them, grown.

And why had she never noticed the way he looked at her, the light in his deep blue eyes reflecting the emotion she had just felt when he touched her?

Oh, Rabbie.

She groped for his hand across the surface of the stiff white sheet that covered her. He captured her fingers in his big, warm ones and held tight.

"Rabbie."

"Lisbeth, you near frightened the life from me." What did she hear in his voice, deep and musical, that caressed her? That same tenderness she saw in his eyes?

Why had she never guessed? She sighed deeply. There had always been Declan.

Rab leaned forward, and the black hair slid over his brow. Lisbeth fought a strong and unprecedented desire to brush it back.

"What happened?" he asked.

She watched his lips, wondered what it would be like to feel them on hers. By the holy heaven, what had come over her?

"I saw him again—Declan. I tried to follow him. I think I fell."

Trouble invaded the deep blue eyes. "I feared 'twas something like that."

"Where am I?"

"Doc Stevens'. You lay out in the rain all night."

"I hurt all over." So she did, as if she'd taken a thrashing.

Doctor Stevens appeared in the doorway behind Rabbie. "Ah, I thought I heard voices. Mrs. O'Shea, how do you feel?"

"I ache a bit. My head—"

"You struck it when you went down. I could find no other injuries. My main concern was getting you warm, for you were out in that rain a long time. How are you in your mind?" He slanted a look at Rab. "Does she seem rational to you?"

Rab hesitated, and Lisbeth wondered if he thought about what she had just told him. Could he possibly consider her seeing her dead husband rational? But he nodded, the black hair spilling forward again.

"Well, Mrs. O'Shea, and what took you out in the rain?"

"I had a dream." Lisbeth's gaze clung to Rab's.

"Do you often walk in your sleep?"

"No, Doctor. Never before."

Doc Stevens frowned. "I dislike the idea of you up the shore on your own, Mrs. O'Shea. I do not believe you've been taking good care of yourself; rather I find you too thin and overworked."

"Don't worry." Rab spoke before Lisbeth could. "She will no' be going back there, not right away. She'll stay for a time here in Lobster Cove."

"Is that so, Mrs. O'Shea?"

Lisbeth's gaze still linked with Rab's, she nodded.

"Very well, then. There's only to finish getting you warm before I release you. I prescribe a roaring fire and a hearty meal."

"Thank you, Doctor."

Stevens went out, and Rabbie began to caress Lisbeth's fingers again. In a low voice he said, "I can no' bear to think of you in that cottage alone, Lisbeth."

"But where will I stay? At Mrs. Taylor's?"

"Nay, wi' me."

Her eyes went wide and color flooded her cheeks. "That is scarcely proper."

"You can live in my quarters; I will stay elsewhere."

"Where?"

"Does it matter? I will find a bunk, never fear. Better me living rough than you."

"I don't wish to put you out. I can stay a few days with Frannie."

"She has no' the room. I want you at my place, Lisbeth, where I know you're safe. Let me do this for you."

She read again what lay in his eyes, and nodded. She was not sure how she felt about the way Rabbie Sinclair regarded her nor why she'd never before caught any hint of it. But oh, it made her feel so secure.

And she needed so badly to feel secure, if only for a time.

****

"There, get yourself around the outside of that." Rabbie plopped a large bowl of stew into Lisbeth's hands—far more than she could eat in three days. She didn't say so. She sat where he had put her, in the best seat in the house—an overstuffed armchair made shabby and comfortable with years of use. She had a blanket over her knees, and Kelpie lay stretched at her feet.

Lisbeth tried to imagine Rabbie lounging in this chair after a hard day's work, alone save for the dog. His quarters behind the forge weren't large and certainly weren't fancy, but they were warm. A fire roared in the hearth, and comfort seemed to settle around Lisbeth's shoulders like a second blanket.

"It's nice here," she surprised herself by saying. She had been in the forge many times, but back here only once or twice. She'd felt a bit intimidated by Tip Howard, though Rabbie always insisted he had a good heart.

Definitely bachelor's quarters, not overly neat or organized, belongings scattered about, haphazard. The bed, little more than an oversized cot, lay in the far corner. Yes, she would sleep warm tonight.

And would Declan follow her even here? She wondered.

Rab filled a second bowl of stew for himself and put a third down for Kelpie, who promptly abandoned Lisbeth.

She smiled and took a spoonful of stew. "Good."

"As you can imagine, a fellow my size does not go hungry often." Rab perched on a stool and dug into his portion.

Lisbeth eyed him. Large he might be, but all muscle. She knew that for fact, having seen him working in his leather apron many a time. Now, for some unaccountable reason, the thought made her grow warm, even more so than should be caused by the blanket.

Firmly she told herself it had been a long time since she'd been in such intimate circumstances with a man. Despite what she saw, or imagined she saw, in Rabbie's eyes, he was above all else her friend. She needed to remember that.

"Have you found a place to sleep?" she asked. He had left her at Doc Stevens' until the good doctor declared himself satisfied with her condition, and returned later to collect her.

"Aye. I'll just bunk in the stable down the street. Tom Bennett says he does no' mind."

Lisbeth wrinkled her nose. "That does not seem right."

"Och, I've slept in much worse places. Anyway, it has a great advantage: Tom is often in and out at all hours and will be able to testify I'm *there* and not *here*."

"Are you so worried about my reputation?"

"I am that worried about any number of things. Tell me again what happened last night."

Lisbeth lowered her spoon. "I was ready for bed, sitting up by the fire." Unable, quite, to make herself go to bed alone. "I heard the wind come up and the rain start. Perhaps I fell asleep, I am not sure. I heard the latch on the door lift. It swung open, and he stood there. *Declan*."

Rab said nothing. Lisbeth searched his eyes and tried to determine what he thought.

Eventually he said gently, "You might have been still asleep—dreaming."

It was what she had told the doctor, and how could she say it was not so? She had dreamed of Declan often.

Helplessly, she shook her head.

"You know, lass, you should keep the bar on the door when you are out there alone."

She asked, because she must, "If he's a ghost, how could he lift the latch?"

"There is no ghost!"

"Never say you don't believe in them, given your highland sensibilities."

"I canno' say that. But in this case I think the only ghost is the one that haunts your mind—your heart.

54

Lisbeth, maybe all this is a sign you need to put your grieving behind you once and for all."

That echoed what Declan had said in her dream: *Go about your life*. Was that the message he brought from his watery grave? Was she to take up her life, perhaps with Rabbie?

The thought half shocked and half thrilled her. She'd never thought of her good friend that way.

Now that she'd seen what lay in his eyes, though, she couldn't seem to think of anything else.

Chapter Nine

"I wish to walk out to the cottage this morning," Lisbeth told Rab as she stirred the porridge.

He had come by early to build up the fire in the forge, and she had called him in to breakfast, the least she could do, she felt, after chasing him from his home.

He stood in the doorway now, clad in his working costume of heavy trousers and leather apron, the black hair tumbling down his neck.

"Nay, Lisbeth," he said. "Not a good idea, that."

"I need to collect Mignon's gown so I can get it finished by Saturday. If she pays me, I will be able to give you back what you lent me, and also put something down at Beatty's. Then I can buy my own groceries."

Rab frowned but said nothing. The frown, she decided, did not suit him.

"Besides," she went on quickly, "it looks to prove a pretty day, and I'd like the exercise."

"Why not let me go get the dress later when I am finished in the forge?"

"Because you've already done enough for me. And, Rab, I'm feeling fine."

"Are you, then?" He took a step nearer and his gaze seared her face; Lisbeth immediately went breathless.

What in heaven's name had come over her? She

had never before focused on things like the breadth of Rabbie Sinclair's shoulders or the length of his black eyelashes—or imagined how that Scots burr might sound in the dark. Disconcerting, to harbor those thoughts and feelings toward one of her best friends.

Could he see what lay in her eyes? Perhaps so, for he took another step closer and raised his hand to cup her cheek. The heat of him enwrapped her, along with a barrage of masculinity.

"I like having you here," he said softly. "Say you're not thinking of moving back out to that place."

"I cannot stay here forever."

"Why not?" Sudden heat flared in his eyes. He bent forward; his fingers caressed her chin, tipped her face up toward his descending mouth.

The first kiss came in but a whisper that brushed her forehead. The second blessed her cheek. Lisbeth tilted her head so the third landed on her lips.

Curiosity made her do it, she told herself. The desire to know. But oh, the sweetness as his warm lips met hers! The softest gift it was—affection rather than demand—yet sensation speared through her like a spring tide.

Lovemaking with Declan had been—well, lovemaking with Declan. He acted always as if he did her a favor by bestowing his attentions, and he demanded his due in return. As his wife, she was expected to pleasure him as he required. Whether she received pleasure in return never seemed uppermost in his mind. For the most part, his charm ended at the bedroom door.

She had adored him so much it never mattered. It had been enough that he belonged to her and her alone;

he had chosen her to be his bride.

Now, through the gentle touch of lips on lips, she felt love come streaming, and it moved her as Declan never had.

"Rabbie."

Did she speak his name into his mouth or only think it? Suddenly the pressure of his lips increased, still making no demand but wooing, persuading. She stretched up on her tiptoes and felt his arms close around her, and draw her home.

When it ended she found both her fists clutched the edges of his apron, fingers brushing his naked chest. The mad idea came into her head: he might lift her in his arms and carry her to the bed in the corner. He might remove her clothing a piece at a time and then his own, the two of them naked together without shame.

For there would never be any shame with this man, only safety and warmth and, perhaps, bliss beyond imagining.

"Rab, you in?" Someone called from the shop: a customer. Rab groaned and tightened his arms around Lisbeth. He rested his forehead against hers.

"Damn! I have been waiting more than ten years for that."

"Have you?"

"Oh, aye."

She loosened her fingers from the smock and ran them up his shoulders, delighting in the warmth and strength of muscle. Her fingertips tingled.

"Why did you never say?"

His gaze met hers, rueful yet honest. "How could I? There was always—"

"Sinclair!"

Whoever had entered the shop drew closer. Hastily, Rab released Lisbeth and stepped away, taking all that marvelous warmth with him, and hurried out to the forge. She turned to find the porridge had stuck fast to the bottom of the pan.

Hastily, she drew it from the heat, listening all the while to the sound of Rab's voice, now speaking to his customer. In her head, she finished the sentence he had begun to her: *there was always Declan O'Shea.* And it was true; since the first time Lisbeth set eyes on Declan, she had never looked at another man.

That didn't mean she should have missed seeing how one of her best friends felt about her.

Suddenly she wished she could go back in time and live it all again: not Declan's death, no—if in fact he was dead, which she found she no longer quite believed. But if she could only see it all, not with a girl's eyes but a woman's, catch the beginnings of what it seemed Rabbie did feel. What then?

It had always been about whether Declan would choose her, but what if she should have been the one making the choice?

****

The gift of sweet kisses Rab had bestowed seemed to travel with Lisbeth as she walked north along the coast path to the cottage. On such a fine day the journey did not seem arduous or long. On her right the rocks fell away to the wide expanse of Frenchman Bay, glittering in the sun. It looked so mild and calm she could barely imagine it raging in storm.

Declan had always called the sea his mistress. "Treacherous she is, lass, and will turn on you in an instant. But sure, she is an exciting ride."

Declan loved excitement. Even at rest—a rare enough state for him—he'd retained a bright gleam in his tawny eyes. What was it about Declan O'Shea that had seized hold of her heart and mind and refused to let go?

Given some distance, it seemed like a magic spell. For she acknowledged now, ruefully, Declan O'Shea had a kind of rough magic about him that had seduced and held her like a dream.

Had those kisses Rab bestowed in his kitchen awakened her? She could not say, yet suddenly everything looked different. A part of her heart would always belong to Declan, but that heart now ached to love again.

The cottage came in sight, perched above its sea wall with the strip of shingle beyond, and white gulls plundering the shore. She quickened her step and, when she drew near enough, saw to her surprise the door stood open.

Ah, but she must have neglected to close it when she ran out after Declan into the night.

Out after Declan.

She cursed softly and hoped the wet would not have blown in, and that Mignon's gown had not suffered damage.

Had Declan truly been here? Had he returned in the flesh, from the sea? If so, why had no one else seen him? Why didn't he make his presence known in daylight?

She shouldered the door open more fully and went in. Damp stained the wooden planks just past the threshold, but all else lay as she had left it. Mignon's gown made a splash of color on the bench, still neatly folded.

The color of Rab's eyes.

Why think of him here, where she'd only ever thought of Declan: thought, lived, and breathed him?

Slowly, she walked around the cottage, marking things she and Declan had shared—the china bowl covered with tiny rosebuds Frannie had given them for their wedding, the kettle that had once belonged to Declan's ma. She gathered items she would need at Rab's, however long she stayed—*how long would she stay?*—her hairbrush, hairpins, and other items only a woman would require.

All the while, through the open door, the sea retained a presence—the quiet hiss and shush of the waves murmuring like a lullaby. Did the sea truly give even as it took? Sustenance given—life taken. Did it, like Declan himself, weave a spell? Had she any hope of escaping it? For with Declan gone she might eventually put her grief behind her and, just possibly, reach for the promise she saw in Rab Sinclair's eyes. But what escape could there be, if Declan remained alive?

She paused at the center of the room and closed her eyes, praying to the great, mystical presence outside her door.

Let me have an answer. Let me know if my heart may be free to love again.

The pure fancy of it made her smile ruefully. She moved on to the doorway of her bedroom, hesitated an instant before moving in. Her eyes fell on a splash of bright yellow in the center of the bed.

A crumpled sou'wester lying like a yellow bird, slain.

Chapter Ten

"Nay, lad, hold it like this. And put some power behind those blows."

Dougie looked at Rab doubtfully. True, Rab reflected, the boy didn't have a lot of power in his stringy body—yet. Just like the skill, that would come.

Dougie choked up on the handle of the hammer and swung a bit wildly, face shining with sweat and strain. His first time beating the hot iron found him far from ready for it. But Rab remembered all too well the frustration of being assigned the work of a dogsbody with no chance at wreaking the magic. Besides, the lad needed to know just how hard the work was, in the forge.

Would Dougie stick with it? Too early to tell, but after only a couple of days Rab saw how he applied himself. He didn't learn easily; neither did he shy away from repetition.

"There now, Dougie," Rab said encouragingly. "You beat on that another half hour or so, and you'll have done a respectable job."

Dougie released the hammer and scrutinized the palm of his hand. "Mr. Sinclair, sir, can I ask you a question?"

"You can." What would it be? How long would it take for the pain in his hands to subside? The ache in his shoulders?

But the boy looked into Rab's face and said, "Why do you call me 'Doogie'? My ma calls me 'Duggie.' That's my name."

Rab smiled. "Well now, 'Doogie' is how we would say your name back in Scotland, from whence I came. 'Tis a common name there, and all."

"Where's Scotland?"

"Over the other side of that ocean out there. Didn't Miss Cooper teach you that?"

Dougie shook his head and wiped his sore hand on his britches surreptitiously.

"She sure talks a lot, does Miss Cooper, but sometimes I find it hard to listen."

"You listen here well enough."

"I like it here. When did you come away from that place—Scotland? Why?"

"I was about your age, maybe a little older." Rab stoked the fire with unconscious skill and gazed back in his mind. The lad who had left Sutherland never dreamed of what his life would become.

"Where was your father?" Dougie asked.

"He died, and my ma along with him, as well as my three wee sisters." His very existence gone to the kirkyard, piece by impossible piece. Even his Border Collie, Gyp.

He turned his eyes on Kelpie who, as ever, lay within reach, and the big Newfoundland swatted the floor with his tail in response. He should have sent Kelpie up the shore with Lisbeth. Why had he let her go alone?

Finishing the tale, he told Dougie, "I had not the means to stay on our croft alone. An uncle paid my passage, out of kindness, he said." Had it been, though?

63

Would it not have been kinder for Uncle Angus to take Rab in, let him stay where the remnants of his heart lay? Angus had said opportunity lay over the water, so the last of Rab's ties had been ruthlessly cut.

"I don't have no father." Dougie announced it with a hint of defiance, effectively interrupting Rab's thoughts.

He reached out and ruffled Dougie's hair. "Everyone has a father, lad."

"Not one I know. My ma says she's not sure who he was." Shame stained the boy's skin darker. A source of agony to him, was it?

Rab remembered Declan and his brother Pat tormenting Rab more than once about his lack of family and his shabby clothes, at least back before Rab grew big enough to stop the taunts. Tip Howard hadn't spared much thought for Rab's appearance. But he'd provided all the food a boy could want and, aye, a rudimentary form of love.

"In the tavern," Dougie went on, speaking more than he had since Rab met him, "they say he was a Penobscot. That's why I look the way I do—different from Timmy. Different from *everybody*."

Bless Emily Cooper, Rab thought, for sending the lad to him. "Nothing wrong with that, lad, if 'tis true."

"But people call them 'dirty Indians.' "

"People say all sorts of things that aren't true."

"But Mr. Sinclair, if I do have a father, why wouldn't he come and see me, not once?"

"Ah, Dougie, there could be a host of reasons. Maybe he doesn't feel he'd be welcome. Maybe," he added delicately, "he never knew about you."

"Oh."

"The important thing to remember, lad, is that you will make the man you become." Just as Rab had after he landed on this rocky shore alone. "'Tis not easy, but it is an opportunity, if you have the courage to see it that way."

Dougie nodded and glanced at his palms again. "This is an opportunity, ain't it?"

"Aye, lad."

Rab hesitated. He had no wish to ask too much from this boy who began to trust him, but he ached to know one more thing. For he sensed he would have to convince Lisbeth of Declan's true nature, if he stood a chance of truly winning her heart.

The kiss they had shared earlier still burned through him, a lingering sweetness that made him desire her all the more.

"Tell me, Dougie, does wee Timmy's father ever come round?"

Dougie raised serious dark eyes. "No, sir."

"So you've no idea either who he is?"

"Folks in the Hogshead say ma's a tramp and will sleep with anyone—they say it behind her back and to her face."

And, Rab thought, some things went beyond the need for proof; Timmy's eyes branded him true. What concerned Rab was the timing of it: the bairn was of an age to show Declan had stepped out on Lisbeth during their marriage.

He asked gently, "How old is Timmy?"

"Four months."

Four months. Conceived when Declan was wed to Lisbeth, then. *The bastard.*

He grimaced and took up the hammer. "Here, lad,

let me show you again how 'tis done."

****

Lisbeth returned shortly before Dougie left for home and just ahead of the dark. Rab breathed a sigh of relief as she passed through the forge on her way to his quarters with Mignon's gown in her arms and a sling pack over her shoulder.

Kelpie abandoned Rab to follow her inside. By the time Rab bid Dougie goodbye and joined them, she had supper started.

And just like that, after only one look at her, Rab knew something was wrong. He could sense her discord and see the distress in her eyes even though they refused to meet his.

"What's amiss?" he asked.

"I brought some things from the cottage and will make supper. I want to repay you as I can."

"You've no need to repay me, Lisbeth. Surely you know that."

She bit her lip. "I must, somehow. Rab, I cannot stay here."

Rab's heart sank abruptly. All day long he had relived the morning's kiss and, if he were honest, hoped for a repetition—if not more. He wanted her so badly he ached. But now he feared he had unaccountably lost ground.

"But you can," he denied it. "All's still right and proper with me sleeping down the street."

Her eyes did lift to his then; blue-gray and dreamy as the sea on a still day, they nevertheless seared him. "How I feel about you is not proper."

Rab promptly lost all the breath in his body. "And how do you feel about me?"

Her gaze moved over him slowly where he stood leaning against the door jamb, lingering on his arms, the muscles of his half-bare chest, and still longer on his mouth.

"I dare not say."

He unpropped himself and moved closer. "Lisbeth, lass, if you are ruing what happened between us this morning, you should no'. It has been a year; you ha' been a widow long enough."

"But I am not a widow," she said.

Chapter Eleven

"I need to show you something." Lisbeth's hands shook as she turned away from the supper preparations to her pack, which lay on the bed. She drew out Declan's sou'wester and stood an instant before turning to face the man who stood behind her. She held the hat out to him like an offering.

Bemusement filled Rab's eyes. His gaze moved from the hat to Lisbeth's face, questioning. "What is that?"

Lisbeth's lips trembled as she spoke. "I found it in the cottage, lying on our bed. Declan's."

Rab did not move except to shake his head. "I do no' understand."

"It's part of his gear. He had this with him the last time he put out in the *White Gull*."

Breath escaped between Rab's lips; his gaze flew to hers once more. "Nay."

"The two times I saw him, Rab—when he appeared during the storm and when I followed him along the track—his head was bare. Bare and wet." She pictured him again, red hair sodden and dripping as if he'd just come out of the sea. "Now this is left for me to find."

Thoughts moved visibly in Rab's blue eyes, denial foremost among them. "It must have been there all the while. You're mistaken about him taking it with him that day."

"It has been there all this time, has it, and I did not notice it on the bed?"

"Well then, someone is playing a cruel joke. 'Tis not Declan's."

"Who would do such a thing to me?" Lisbeth had contemplated the question all the way back to town. "Anyway, it is his. Look." She turned the sou'wester in her fingers, showing Rab where it had been rent and mended. "He caught it on a nail. I know my own stitches."

"Sweet heaven!" Rab looked precisely the way Lisbeth felt, as if he'd received a physical blow. He took the sou'wester from her and touched the ridge of stitching with his thumb. "But how can it be?"

"I have been over and over it," she said, "searching for an explanation. This may have washed up with the pieces of the *White Gull*—if so, someone found it and waited all this time to, as you say, play a cruel joke. Or, Declan left it on the bed."

"From the afterlife, you mean? The spirit world?"

And there spoke the highlander, Lisbeth thought. She smiled grimly. "No. I saw him, Rabbie. I know you don't believe me, but I know, too, what I beheld with my own eyes. Declan must be alive."

Rab swayed where he stood. "Nay," he said again. "If so, where's he been all this while? Why would he no' come forward?"

The very same questions Lisbeth had asked herself. Declan couldn't be alive, yet her heart insisted he was.

Her heart knew a wealth of other things also: she no longer wanted to live in the numb dream state she seemed to have inhabited since Declan's supposed demise. She wanted to take her life into her own hands.

And she had feelings—powerful ones—for this man who stood before her. Yet he was not Declan. And if Declan lived, she remained still his wife.

"Here—sit." Rab clasped her hand and drew her onto the edge of his cot. "How sure are you the man you saw was Declan?"

"Sure." A woman knew her husband even after he had supposedly been a year in the sea.

"When he made these appearances, did he say anything to you?"

"My name." *Lisbeth*, in a gurgle—not with that crooning, Irish lilt he'd sometimes used in the dark.

Again the thoughts moved in Rab's eyes. He released Lisbeth's fingers and formed his hands into fists which he rested on his knees.

"But lass, if 'tis Declan, why would he stay a year away from you?"

"I don't know. I've a mind to go back up there and stay until he appears again so I can ask him."

Rab stiffened in protest. "Better I go instead."

"He may not come if you're there. It may be me he wants to see."

"Over my dead body will you go back out there alone." Rab grimaced. "Sorry, Lisbeth—a bad choice of words, that."

Lisbeth studied him. "Before you saw that hat, you believed I imagined all this."

"I did not know what to believe. Declan always had such a hold on your heart."

"On all of me." Lisbeth began to see that now, like a woman truly waking from a dream—or a spell. From the first moment she met Declan back in school, she had been unable to turn her eyes away.

"Magic," she whispered. "Declan had a kind of magic." Grimly she corrected herself, "*Has* a kind of magic."

Soberly, Rab nodded. "And as we know from the old tales, lass, magic can sometimes deceive."

Lisbeth's gaze flew to his. What did she see in his eyes? Rueful reluctance? Certainty... "Why do you say that?"

He drew a breath that expanded his deep chest. "Lisbeth, I would have you consider Declan may not have been what he seemed. I know"—he held up a hand—"how you idolized him. The sun rose and set on him for you. But the man was far from perfect."

"I know that." Lisbeth had been well aware of Declan's faults, the primary one of which was his selfishness. It and it alone motivated nearly all he did. But that ceased to matter once he gave her his wide grin burgeoning with charm, and spoke to her in that Irish brogue, calling her "Lisbeth, mine." It had ceased to matter when he chose her and her alone out of the flock of women who pursued him. He might have smiled at them all, danced attention on them all, but he'd married Lisbeth Parsons. Didn't that prove his heart could love?

He'd stayed selfish during the year of their marriage, often going off to drink with his brother and pals on fine days when he should have been hauling traps, neglecting chores about the cottage like his father before him. Fortunately, they'd had what Lisbeth earned, sewing, upon which to fall back.

Indeed, she thought now, the wonder was that Declan had put out to sea that fatal day, one that threatened storm.

Seriously, she told Rab, "I am not a fool."

"Aye, you are not, which makes it more surprising you could no' see the truth."

"If you have something to say, Rabbie Sinclair, out with it. Do not dance about."

"I have reason to believe Declan was no' faithful to you in your marriage."

Lisbeth caught her breath, as at a blow. Not that! The unwelcome thought had appeared from time to time in her mind, but she had always pushed it away firmly. He had married her, and the marriage vows had to mean something. They had taken them together in St. Joseph's, the church of his faith. Declan would always be *Declan*, but there had been a streak of devoutness running through him, the same that led him to cross himself before he went to sea and refuse to take the Lord's name in vain.

Yet Lisbeth knew Rabbie Sinclair for a man honest to the bone.

"What reason have you to believe this?" she asked.

For the first time, Rab's gaze fell from hers. Reluctantly he said, "There were rumors both before and after you wed."

"I never heard them."

"Folk were no' likely to bring such a thing to your ears, were they? They spoke in whispers. Declan was not always where he should be. No one wanted to hurt you." Implied in the words was the meaning: he, Rab, had not.

Distress pierced Lisbeth to the heart. As if sensing her emotions, Kelpie came and rested his chin on her knees. Unthinking, she caressed his big head.

"Proof," she said. "I will need proof."

Rab's gaze returned to hers. "There may be some."

Chapter Twelve

"You've done a lovely job." Mignon La Marche held up the blue gown and scrutinized it with her shrewd hazel eyes. "Were you able to let out the seams as I asked?"

"Yes."

"Then let me try it on and make sure it fits before you go."

And pay me, Lisbeth added silently. She'd walked all the way out to Mignon's grand house on the bluff—no short trek from Rabbie's forge—and delivered the gown the day before the dance, as promised.

"Would you like some tea while you wait?" Mignon asked, very offhand. "I'll tell the maid."

Stiffly, Lisbeth shook her head. She had to admit she felt uncomfortable standing here in the opulent parlor with its damask draperies and red velvet furniture. Back when they'd been girls together, Mignon had always held herself as just that little bit superior to Lisbeth and Frannie. Yet who would have thought then she would land, like a jewel, in this setting?

But she had wed a wealthy man, while Lisbeth had taken in marriage the near-penniless lobster fisherman with the shabby cottage and the reluctance to work even when he should. True, back then Mignon had wanted Declan too, had rarely left off following him with her eyes or seeking to engage him in conversation.

Strange how things turned out, she thought as Mignon hurried from the room with the gown in her hands.

She crossed to the parlor windows and looked out. The room commanded a fine view out over the cliffs and across the south end of Frenchman Bay. On a clear day like this one, it seemed she could see forever.

And did Declan's bones lie there beneath all that blue water? Had she dreamed about seeing him after all? But no; she'd held his sou'wester in her hands.

She shivered, the spasm passing down her spine long and slow. For all its grandeur, this big house seemed far too silent and empty. She didn't know how Mignon stood it here alone.

Upon that thought she heard a creak as of a foot on a loose floorboard, and spun to face the door. No one there; she had to get hold of her nerves, she thought impatiently.

The ticking of the case clock in the corner grew deafening before Mignon returned. She entered the room still smoothing her rich, auburn hair and gave Lisbeth a smile.

"It fits very well. Now I shall just have to refrain from comforting myself too often with biscuits. Of course after I wear the gown at the dance tomorrow, it won't much matter, will it?"

All those stitches, all the hours spent, Lisbeth thought, and Mignon meant to wear the gown but once.

And where was the coin Lisbeth had been promised? They'd had a deal, fine lady or no. Surely Mignon did not mean to make her ask.

Lisbeth straightened her spine even as he cheeks

grew warm. "I am glad you're pleased with my work."

"It's fine, thank you."

"There is the small matter of payment."

"But surely I paid you when I ordered the gown."

"You gave me the cost of the fabric which I ordered, yes. You promised the rest upon completion."

Mignon tipped her head, studying Lisbeth thoughtfully. "Are you certain?"

"Quite certain, Mignon. Do you not remember you tried to give me the gown in payment?"

"I do not recall. Not trying to double charge me, are you? No, of course you wouldn't—not an honest woman such as Lisbeth O'Shea. What was the agreed price?"

Lisbeth named it, lips stiff and cheeks now flaming.

"Wait another moment."

Mignon went out, and Lisbeth caught an additional whisper of sound from the foyer beyond. Did Mignon speak to someone? Her maid, surely.

Mignon returned quickly this time, with a small purse. Careful as a miser, she counted out the coins and dropped them one by one into the palm of Lisbeth's hand, which now trembled.

"There you go. I hope you will do a job or two for me again."

Lisbeth longed to refuse and knew she could not. Mignon's was the best custom she could hope to get in Lobster Cove.

She nodded, still stiffly.

Mignon tipped her head again. "Funny how things work out, isn't it?" she asked whimsically, echoing Lisbeth's earlier thoughts. "So many of us who were at

75

school together ended up orphaned—Pat and Declan, when their parents died, then my father soon after. Your parents died on that journey back to St. John's, and Rab arrived here an orphan. Only Frannie has a parent to her name. And now you and I are widowed, as well! It's a hard berth in Lobster Cove."

Not so hard for Mignon, Lisbeth thought bitterly as she tucked the precious coins into her pouch. Had Mignon loved her husband or only his fortune and position? An unkind question that, she admitted ruefully.

To Mignon she said, "We all manage as we can."

She turned to leave, but Mignon stopped her with a question. "Have you decided to attend the dance?"

"Most likely not. I am staying at Rab's—"

"I know." Mignon's eyes brightened with malice. "It's the talk of the town."

"Is it?" Lisbeth paused in consternation. The last thing she wanted was to complicate Rab's life. "But he is not staying there."

"Not at night, perhaps. But night is not the only time for a man and woman to get up to what they may, together. You of all women should know that—married to Declan O'Shea."

Lisbeth's eyes narrowed. How did Mignon guess Declan had demanded the occasional afternoon in bed when he should have been out working?

"Rab is a decent man. If my staying there is damaging his reputation, I will move out."

"Um-hm. His reputation, is it, and not your own? You always were so straight-laced, Lisbeth. I could never guess what Declan saw in you, and him such a wild lad."

"Opposites attract."

"And birds of a feather flock—as well as do other things—together." Mignon gave a wicked smile. "Rab is attractive enough. Do you mean to tell me you have never noticed?"

To her discomfiture, Lisbeth felt her cheeks heat again.

When she did not reply, Mignon went on, "Certainly there are other women in Lobster Cove who think so."

"You?" Lisbeth asked, turning sick inside.

Mignon laughed. "No, not quite to my taste is our lad Rab. But I know for a fact Emily Cooper has set her cap at him."

"Oh?"

"Heard she makes excuses to go to his shop, and also asked him to the dance."

"Rab has taken on one of her students for apprentice—that's why she was there."

"Oh, Lisbeth, I think not. True, she's no beauty, but she has a fine head on her shoulders and is obviously a woman who knows what she wants."

"I must go."

"I will walk you out. Such a fine day! I hope the weather holds for tomorrow. Here, let me show you something. Have you ever seen the view from the cliffs?"

Reluctantly, Lisbeth followed as Mignon took the path from the front door toward the rocks that overlooked the ocean. A slight wind blew inshore, bringing the scents Lisbeth always associated with Declan: salt and the slight tang of fish. The sun, nearly overhead, cast dazzling patterns of light on the water, and Lisbeth could hear the hiss and drag of waves far below.

"Beautiful," she said, because it was.

"This view is why Claude wanted to build here. He did me a favor—more than he ever knew." A faraway look came to Mignon's eyes as she remembered her husband.

"Did you love him?" Lisbeth dared ask.

"Claude?" Mignon cast her a look. "Not the way you loved Declan, perhaps. But there was affection, yes, and gratitude."

Lisbeth wondered what it had been like, bedding a man so old—Claude had been sixty—but she certainly wouldn't ask that.

"I must go," she said again.

Mignon ignored her. "Oh, look! A white gull—of what does that remind you?" Mignon asked, and shot another glance at Lisbeth. "And look, did you know there's a path just here? See that gap between the rocks?"

Dutifully, Lisbeth leaned forward and peered down. She would not like to have to make that nearly vertical descent. "Why would anyone want to go down there?" she wondered aloud.

"When the tide is out, there's a narrow strip of shingle below. Not now, of course. Careful!" Mignon grabbed at Lisbeth's shoulder. "Do not lean too far; you might fall, and that would no doubt be the end of you."

Lisbeth took a decided step backwards. "Yes. Thank you for your custom, Mignon. I hope you enjoy the dance."

"I am sure I will."

Lisbeth walked away quickly and took the coast

path northward. All the way back to Lobster Cove, she tried to convince herself that when Mignon caught her shoulder she hadn't urged Lisbeth forward, instead of pulling her back from the edge.

Chapter Thirteen

"Good afternoon to you, Rab. We do not see you in here often."

"Afternoon, Sam," Rab returned, and nodded to the proprietor of the Hogshead. "Warm day, in the forge. I fancied a pint of your best."

Sam gave a gap-toothed smile. "My best is very good indeed." He pulled the pint almost before Rab pushed up to the bar. "And if I worked half as hard as you do, I'd be in here every day."

"I work hard enough to keep from drinking up all my profits," Rab told him equably. It was one of the first lessons Tip Howard had imparted. Not that Tip objected to a drink now and then. He just kept his own bottle of rum in the kitchen cupboard.

"Remember, lad," he'd said more than once, "hot metal and the drink don't mix."

Now Rab took a deep draught from the mug Sam set before him and glanced around the room. He had hoped Maggie Grier might be on the job, but the place was nearly empty at this hour of the afternoon. In fact, school would let out soon, and Dougie would be at the forge. Rab had limited time.

Sam, apparently in the mood to talk, leaned his elbows on the bar. "You going to the dance tomorrow?"

"Me, dance?" Rab returned as he had to Emily Cooper. "'Tisn't a pretty sight, that."

"Thought you might intend to take your new ladybird."

"Eh? What's that?"

"The Widow O'Shea. Heard you two are a couple now."

Rab froze with the glass half way to his lips. "Where did you hear that?"

"It's all over town. And about time, too. She's a sweet thing and terrible young to be left without a husband. Be fine if she married again."

Rab's heart began to pound in his chest. "Is that what folk think? That we're bound to marry?" All he'd ever wanted since he first laid eyes on Lisbeth all those years ago.

"No reason not to, is there? You're a decent man and she's a respectable woman—not like some I could name—so marriage seems only natural."

"We have not got to that point. Yet." Rab leaned on the bar also. "Can I ask you something Sam, just between the two of us?"

Sam's brown eyes, steady and kind, met Rab's. "You can."

"What did you know about Declan O'Shea? His behavior before he died, I mean. His—character."

Sam's gaze cooled a whit. "Everybody knew what Declan was—everybody except that little wife of his, maybe, and her stuck out there up the shore."

"Just what was he?"

Sam lowered his voice even though no one was near enough to overhear. "Do I have to say it?"

"Please."

"You went to school with him. You must know."

Aye, Rab knew. Declan lived by his own rules and

got away with whatever he could. In school, if he could not dodge a quiz he cheated on it. A smile and a wink and a beguiling look from those tawny eyes usually brought him dispensation.

Baldly, Rab asked, "Did he step out on his wife?"

"Well, now." Sam directed a hard look at him. "That's a curious question."

"I'm a curious man."

"You're not, though. I should have said, Rab Sinclair, you're a man who keeps his nose in his own business—conspicuous for it."

But Lisbeth Parsons O'Shea was Rab's business: if what he suspected proved true, he should have moved to protect her years ago.

He gave Sam a shrug. "It's something I've wondered about for a long time."

"Well, wonder no more. In my job it pays to be discreet, but what can it matter now? The man's dead."

"So—how many? And when?"

"Son, Declan O'Shea went through women the way some men go through pints. Don't know if he was standing stud to them all, but he enjoyed their company, loved charming them and stealing at least a kiss or two. I've seen him at work in this very room."

"Your barmaid, Maggie?" Rab inquired.

"Well, now, why ask questions if you already know the answers?"

"When was this?" The most pertinent piece of information, that. "The reason I ask is, I've taken the woman's son for apprentice, and when I went to speak with her I got a look at her other wee bairn."

"Ah."

"He does no' look like his mother, nor his older

82

brother."

Sam's gaze met Rab's again, frankly this time. "Looks like his father, he does."

"That's what I suspected."

"Declan O'Shea," Sam said ruefully, "could have seduced a nun. Maggie Grier proved no challenge."

"What about Declan's brother?"

"Pat?"

"Aye, it occurred to me the child could be Pat's. He and Declan looked as alike as two peas from the same pod." Of course, if Rab remembered correctly, Pat O'Shea had brown eyes. Still, he carried the same blood that had bestowed those tawny eyes on Declan.

But Sam shook his head. "If memory serves, Pat was seein' Rachel Tennant back then."

"Could have been walking out with more than one woman. He did take off out of here round about the time Maggie would have come up expecting."

"True, that. I know only what I saw in here. Declan hung about, sometimes when he should have been hauling traps, and Maggie took him back to that place of hers."

"Do you think Maggie would tell the truth of it?"

"Why? What does it matter now? Maggie has two sons by two different men. No one should be surprised."

"Well, the thing is, I would not want Lisbeth clapping eyes on that child, and him the spit of her dead husband."

"You're a considerate man, Rab Sinclair. My advice: marry the woman, give her a child of her own, and make her forget. She's not the first woman in these parts lost a man to the sea."

Rab shrugged and supped some more ale before he asked, "You would not know where Pat O'Shea hared off to, would you?"

"Heard tell he went up to fishing the Grand Banks for the season and after that signed on a sealer. Of course, that was last year. You might get word of him from Billy Dixon. The two of them were tight before Pat went away."

Rab nodded. Billy, who ran his own lobster boat, seemed a steady sort, in his mid-forties, with a wife and a brood of bairns.

"But," he pressed, "you're sure Pat's not been in town?" It had occurred to Rab during the sleepless night just past, lying in the stable prey to his thoughts, Pat might be a likely candidate to impersonate Declan and play a prank on Lisbeth. Appearing suddenly out of the darkness, soaking wet and with Lisbeth already in a state, Pat might well be able to fool her.

But why, after a year? And that did not explain the damned sou'wester.

"I will speak with Billy Dixon as soon as I can."

"How you getting on with Maggie's boy, Dougie?"

"Well enough. The lad's been working hard."

"Decent of you to give him a chance."

"Tip Howard gave me one. Thanks for the drink, Sam, and the information. I'd be pleased if you'd keep what we discussed under your hat."

Sam tipped an invisible cap, and Rab went out into the afternoon.

He had no time now to search out Billy Dixon, likely still at sea. But Rab knew to the roots of his soul he needed to solve this mystery if he wanted any hope of winning Lisbeth's heart.

Chapter Fourteen

The autumn dance, held at the hall adjacent to St. Joseph's, went late Saturday night. Lisbeth could hear the music from Rab's, all the way down First Street: Fred Andrews, she knew, with his fiddle, Henry Drake with his squeezebox, and Tommy O'Brien with a bodhran. They played at all Lobster Cove events, and sounded so lively this night they had Lisbeth tapping her foot when she should be thinking of sleep.

The weather being mild—just as Mignon had hoped—she opened the window in Rab's quarters and leaned out, the better to listen. Rab had already gone off down the street to the stable, and in a right strange mood for himself.

Rab quite obviously had something on his mind. Lisbeth leaned on her elbows, absorbing the sound of the tune "*Si Bheag, Shi Mhor*" afloat on the night air, and wondered about him. He had been late coming to the forge this morning, and when he did appear Lisbeth could see the trouble sitting on his shoulders.

Broad, strong shoulders... Lisbeth blinked determinedly. She had no business thinking about Rabbie that way, how good his arms had felt around her, how good he smelled, or how that kiss from him had tasted. She had no business imagining how it would feel to run her fingers through his black hair, or strip the rough clothing from him a piece at a time.

85

Didn't she more than half believe her husband was still alive? Besides, from the very first there had been no one for her but Declan, Declan, *Declan*. How could she take such delight now in merely thinking about Rabbie Sinclair?

Yet she couldn't seem to do anything else. Leaning there in the soft dark she considered: what if she had, all that while, followed after the wrong man, trailing him the way a child might a will-o-the-wisp?

Now she truly did feel very like a woman wakened from a deep dream. She had started awake that first time she saw Declan in her bedroom doorway, as if back from the stormy sea. And, awakened, she had begun to see things differently.

Honesty demanded she admit it: she wanted a chance with Rab, longed to claim the life she believed he held out to her in his big hands, the promise in his deep, blue eyes.

And that would be simpler if she knew Declan was really dead.

The music from down the street turned lively, a bright slip jig. Giving up the very idea of sleep, Lisbeth slid her shawl around her shoulders and went outside.

She loved Lobster Cove at night, even when the breeze didn't carry a tune. It felt so safe—not fey and lonely like the cottage up the shore. Yet the sea, life's blood of them all, remained within reach. Lisbeth could smell the salt tang and almost catch the sound of the waves.

That ocean had carried her family from England to Newfoundland, had carried Declan's people from Ireland, and had brought the lonely, bereaved lad, Rabbie, from Scotland. It had also carried the *White*

Gull to its doom. For whatever else she imagined, she knew the *White Gull* had come ashore in pieces that night.

Back in the cottage, tucked beneath the bed, lay the ragged length of wood that had washed up that fateful evening last year. The trawler's name, in white on a background of blue, had been painted there by Declan's father some years ago, when he had—quite uncharacteristically—refurbished the boat. Lisbeth the child had gone up the shore that very day he finished it, going as she often did, pretending to gather stones on the shingle but in truth hoping for a glimpse of the wild boy with the red hair and the tawny eyes.

So she could not mistake—the *White Gull* had broken up in that storm. How then could Declan have survived?

She found her feet carrying her, of their own accord, toward the stables. Heading down Maple Street she could see the clouds gathering over the sea— Mignon's good weather might not last long.

Kelpie came out to meet her when she reached the stables. She greeted him softly and ruffled the fur on his great, black head.

"Where's your master, eh? Sleeping?"

"He's here." Rab's deep, lilted voice came at her out of the darkness. She started as he stepped from the shadows. "I could no' sleep," he confessed.

"Nor I." In the dim, soft light she saw he came but half-dressed as he must have lain in his bed: bare feet, a pair of trousers, and a shirt open at the front to reveal his broad chest. His dark hair, well mussed, tumbled down his neck; his eyes gleamed.

She reached for him blindly, like a woman seeking

refuge from storm. His hands closed on hers and she stumbled forward into his arms.

The bliss of it enfolded her even as it had back in his quarters. A wild yearning arose inside her, and she felt his instantaneous response, as if his emotions sensed and answered hers. Despite his size, she fitted perfectly in his arms. Her body melded to his as if they belonged together.

She raised her lips and, after a heartbeat, he claimed them. As before, the caress began gently, a whisper of sensation that tasted of devotion. Then the unrecognized emotion bloomed inside Lisbeth and she knew it for passion.

She parted her lips beneath his, and he dove in. She sighed his name into him as his tongue began to explore her mouth with aching intimacy. With a shock, Lisbeth realized she'd never before tasted this kind of desire.

Then she forgot about her past and what she knew—forgot most miraculously about Declan, who had occupied her thoughts for more than ten years.

For Rab's big, warm hands cradled her; his mouth wooed her. She could feel his heart thudding beneath the muscles of his chest. He tasted of delightful things: the pure, tangy essence of male, irresistible daring—and home.

Why had she never seen that Rabbie Sinclair was her home?

She sighed again and melted into him. He broke the kiss and slid his hands up to cup her face.

"My God, Lisbeth."

"Don't stop, Rabbie. Please don't."

"But—"

She kissed him again, putting her whole heart into

it—the heart that seemed to have so recently awakened from a long, slow dream. He made a sound deep in his throat and, his mouth still on hers, drew her into the stable.

Or perhaps he carried her; Lisbeth could not say her feet still touched the ground. Caught so fast in his arms, she didn't care.

The darkness inside the stable, deep and smelling of hay and horses, wrapped around them. Rab's bed would be close at hand. Lisbeth wanted so badly to be there with him it hurt.

She unclasped her hands from where they had linked around his neck and slid them down his shoulders to his naked chest. Smooth, warm skin met her palms, and lower down a sprinkling of hair that made her fingers itch with delight. She continued to explore until she encountered the waist of his trousers. He grunted, but did not stop kissing her.

Touch me in return, she begged him mentally. As if he heard, he slid one hand from where it cradled her around to her breast. Lisbeth saw stars. Her desire became a law unto itself, a reason to draw breath. She wanted nothing but to be naked beneath this man, alive to his touch, his in body and spirit.

Again she broke the kiss, leaving them both gasping. "Where is your bed?"

"Lisbeth, no. We canna'."

How thick his highland accent became when he was aroused! And oh, he was—Lisbeth could feel the proof of that pressing against her, and it turned any lingering resistance to water.

Even as he protested, his hands explored her clothing, seeking a way inside her bodice—precisely where she wanted him.

She whimpered, "It unbuttons. In back."

His clever fingers found the row of buttons and made short work of them. Her loosened bodice fell forward.

A shiver traveled down Lisbeth's spine, almost as if someone watched them. Just the cool air hitting her overheated flesh, she assured herself. No one could see them here in the dark.

The distant music floating down the street changed to the slow rhythm of a Strathspey, the beat of which seemed to match that of Lisbeth's laboring heart. She shrugged her bodice forward so it fell to her waist, aflame for this man as she had never been before.

He took what she offered, not with his hands but with his mouth. She felt the heat of it slide over her skin in a shower of kisses that ended in a swirl of his tongue at the tip of one breast.

And just like that, she belonged to him. Ah, well, she thought madly, she had been his all the while, she just hadn't known. Now he pressed closer so he could plunder her, and she gave herself to the heat of his mouth, placing her soul in his keeping.

"Beautiful," he murmured, his hot breath gusting against her damp skin. "You ha' always been as beautiful as a star in the heavens."

"Take me to your bed. Please." Lisbeth felt as if liquid fire flowed through her veins, uncontrollable. "Do I have to beg?"

He laughed unsteadily, and her heartbeat tripped up a notch. "I canna'," he protested again.

"Will you deny me, Rab Sinclair? You have never been a cruel man."

"I will deny you nothing, precious lass! Neither will I do anything you may regret."

"I have never wanted anything more than I want you."

"Truly?" That froze him where he stood, hair tumbled over his forehead, one hand caressing her breast. "Even—?"

"Never," she assured him. "Rabbie—"

He gasped like a man under duress; she felt him fight his impulses. "But—you may not be free."

Lisbeth faced that fairly, knew it for truth, and struggled to restrain the demands not of her flesh but of her heart. Could she live with the possibility of breaking her marriage vows? Moreover, could Rab live with it?

Before she could answer, Kelpie growled. The sound rose eerily through the dark stable and made Lisbeth's hair stand on end.

Beneath her hands, Rab tensed.

"Someone is there," he breathed.

Lisbeth turned. Against the lighter darkness of the open doorway she saw a figure silhouetted—one she knew, with wild red hair, a lithe body, squared shoulders, and that stance like no other.

Her husband, Declan O'Shea.

Chapter Fifteen

Kelpie gave a bark and lunged forward. The very last thing Rab wanted was to let go of the woman in his arms. But her gasp told him the identity of the man outlined in the doorway.

As if Rab needed that confirmed.

He released Lisbeth gently and followed in Kelpie's wake. The dog, little more than a blur, hurtled after the man who had stood observing Rab and Lisbeth's embrace. Only, he could not have seen much in the dark, could he? Not unless he truly was a spirit.

Generations of highland superstition made the skin all over Rab's body prickle. Back where he'd been born, they believed in the Second Sight, the veracity of tea leaves, and the occasional return of the dead—especially from the sea. Scotland, a place of rocky shores, deep lochs, and beguiling mist, contained a surfeit of water spirits. Was the dog that loped ahead of him not named for one?

Declan—if this was Declan and not just his spirit—pounded down Maple Street, making straight for the shore. Charging after him, Rab could see a storm had gathered over the ocean, now moving in fast. The three of them ran straight into a rising wind.

He spared a thought for Lisbeth and hoped she would stay at the stables, or go home. He could not hear her coming behind him; he could not hear much with the wind in his ears.

The streets of Lobster Cove lay empty, with most everybody at the dance. No one saw Declan run by, pursued by the great, black dog which appeared to be closing on him, and Rab coming after.

They had nearly reached the harbor when Kelpie leaped—a remarkable act from an animal that had never showed an ort of aggression. Rab saw the man ahead of him stagger, then free his arm from the dog's grip. He did not fall.

"Declan!" Rab bellowed.

The man turned his wild head. Lightning flashed in the clouds behind him. He raised his fist and brought it down on Kelpie's head.

"No!" Rab shouted.

Declan took off again. Rab now knew in his heart this *was* Declan, who had never liked Kelpie and had sneered at Rab when he accepted the pup in payment for a job done.

"You're nothing but a soft girl, Rab Sinclair," he'd goaded. "Barely a man at all."

Rage now stirred in Rab's heart—as rare as Kelpie's aggression. He longed to catch Declan and complete a confrontation more than ten years overdue.

It would take more than a blow to the head to keep the big Newfoundland down; Kelpie's skull likely barely felt that, Rab thought. Yet he burned with anger; he had never raised a hand to the pup. Damned if anyone else would.

Kelpie started off in pursuit once more, and Rab followed, his heart pounding. The delivery of a blow proved Declan no spirit. But if alive, where had he been for the last year? And where was he bound?

Declan reached Main Street and veered right toward the coast road heading southward. The gathering storm now shut out the starlight, and Rab could barely see the man ahead of him. He quickened his pace, not wanting to lose his quarry.

Kelpie once more bounded ahead, and Rab heard Declan yell. He swore to himself, wishing he could see better. As if in answer, lightning flashed and showed him Kelpie and Declan down on the verge and appearing to wrestle together.

An instant of brightness and the image once more disappeared into the dark. Rab pressed forward and reached the place just as the rain began.

He could hear Declan—or whoever it was—swearing and hollering at the dog.

"Leave go of me, you great bastard! Let me go!"

The voice sounded like Declan's. Rab's head spun and his stomach knotted. All this while, he had wanted to believe Declan O'Shea dead. Some cruel prank, some impersonation, yes—even a spirit, in truth. But he did not want Declan returning to take up his place in Lisbeth's life.

Yet the man struggling on the ground with Kelpie must surely be made of flesh and blood.

"Declan!" he roared into the darkness. "Declan O'Shea?"

The man did not respond, but he gave another yell and broke away from Kelpie with a sound of rending cloth.

Rab swore to himself again; a few more steps and he would have had the culprit.

He heard rather than saw the man run on into the night. The storm now beat at the coast road where he and Kelpie stood; the wind played havoc with Rab's senses. He pressed on but with a sinking heart knew he would not glimpse his quarry again.

So it proved. He and Kelpie walked another half mile, the big dog now keeping close to Rab's side, but even during the flashes of lightning saw no one ahead. Just the empty track and, to their left, rocks and the wild sea rising.

"Come on, lad," Rab called at last. "This is daft."

Declan could have gone anywhere—most likely off the road and inland. Or back to the sea… Impossible to tell.

He and the dog, now both well-wetted, turned back for town. Rab had not gone far when he saw a figure struggling toward him.

This one he did recognize. "Lisbeth! What are you doing out here? Are you mad?"

They met before she answered, and she tumbled forward into his arms.

"Was it him? Was it Declan?"

Aye, and the answer to that question possessed both their minds, even above the storm.

Rab caressed her shoulders with his hands, trying to lend some warmth to her chilled flesh, before he replied.

"I think so. I could no' tell for certain. Come on!"

He tucked her beneath his arm and, with Kelpie hurrying ahead, they fled back to town. Lisbeth did not speak again, but he felt her trembling.

He could no longer hear music coming from the hall, but neither did they meet anyone heading their way. The dancers must all be holed up at the church, out of the rain. A blessing, he thought, as he ushered

Lisbeth into his quarters.

As soon as they got inside she swung to face him. "It must have been Declan. He always comes with a storm!"

"Whisht!" Rab told her. Wet to the skin and white to the lips, she looked like he'd just fished her out of the ocean. "Warm yourself, lass, and put on some dry clothes."

He stirred up the fire before snatching a cloth and going to work on the big Newfoundland's coat.

When he looked up, Lisbeth still stood staring at him. "Where did he go?"

"I could no' tell, love."

"Oh, Rab!" Once again she stumbled forward into his arms. "If it is Declan, why would he do this? Why would he stay so long away from me and play such terrible games now? Where has he been?"

Rab's stomach dropped. *Why would he stay so long away from me?* Was that the cry of Lisbeth's heart? Did she want Declan yet? He tucked her head beneath his chin, and his chest ached. He longed for this woman with every part of his being, but if he loved her, indeed he must want what proved best for her.

Could that be Declan—selfish, feckless, and unfaithful—back in her life?

"He was watching us," she whispered. "He saw us together in the stable, what we were doing."

"List, now." Rab shook her very gently and leaned back to gaze into her eyes. "I will no' have you torturing yourself over that." Of all things. If Declan O'Shea got an eyeful of his wife in the arms of another man, it proved no more than he deserved.

Rab had to find a way to tell Lisbeth about Maggie

Grier. But how? All the words and phrases he formed in his head sounded like attempts to turn her from Declan.

"But—"

"Lisbeth, he could not have seen much, it was far too dark. He may have followed you there—if 'twas he."

"Who else could it have been?"

"I ha' been thinking about that. It might be Pat playing these tricks on us."

"Pat?"

"Aye. You know how alike they were, to look at."

"But he's away."

"Is he?"

"Even if he's come back, Rab—why would he do such a thing?"

"That's what we need to find out. I mean to go looking for Pat. If I find him elsewhere—well, then we will have to think again."

Very gently, he told her, "Now change your clothes. I will change mine in the forge, so you have some privacy."

She nodded. Rab gathered his things and went out into the gloom of the forge, his heart aching. Overhead the storm still raged, but no wilder than the tempest in his blood.

Chapter Sixteen

"I want to come with you to look for Pat O'Shea."

Resolute and insistent, Lisbeth greeted Rab when he arrived at the forge. Behind him, clear morning sunlight spilled across the floor. Last evening's storm had flown half way through the night.

Lisbeth, lying in Rab's bed with the scent of him warm all around her, had not slept. Rab had insisted on leaving Kelpie with her when he returned to the stables. She'd listened to the big dog breathing and then snoring, but her mind refused to quiet.

Now she stood with her hand resting on the Newfoundland's head. Kelpie seemed to understand he'd been assigned to protect her, and he would not stir from her side.

"I do not know where Pat is," Rab replied after giving Lisbeth a searing glance. That look touched her to her soul. Half the agony she endured during the night had centered on the way it felt, being in his arms. How different it was from being with Declan—how deeply Rab moved her, stirred her, made her desire to bond completely with him.

Now he had only to look at her with those deep blue eyes and it heated her blood. What, oh, what, to do with these feelings?

Rab went on, "I mean to speak wi' Billy Dixon. Sam at the Hogshead thinks Billy might know where

Pat's gone."

Or if Pat had returned. Lisbeth contemplated that possibility. Could it have been Pat she saw those two times at the cottage and again last night? Maybe. She could not let herself contemplate anything else.

"When?"

Rab shot her another look. "I hope to see Billy today. He should be going over his boat after last night's blow."

"Then I will come with you."

"Lisbeth, I do no' think 'tis a good idea, that."

"I am tired of playing the grieving widow. If someone's pulling a prank on me, I want to know."

Before he could object further, she ducked back into his quarters and snatched up her shawl. "No time like the present."

Kelpie pacing at Lisbeth's side, the three of them started down toward the harbor, where Lisbeth knew Billy Dixon docked his trawler. Folk were out this morning as they had not been last night, some cleaning up storm damage. They greeted her and Rab as they passed.

Overhead, the cloud cover had cleared as the storm bank slid to the north. Last night felt like a dream—all of it, the terrible chase with her in pursuit of Rab and Kelpie as well as what had come before in the dark stable. Had Rab truly held her with such searing tenderness? Had she kissed him with that wild hunger? Had she bared her breasts for him? Had his hot mouth covered them?

She shivered in response, like a woman with a fever, and Rab glanced at her. "It will be all right," he assured her.

"How can it?"

"You have to believe." He gazed out over the ocean, now turned the deep blue shade of his eyes. "Aye, sometimes it's harder to do that than other times. When I landed here on this shore as a lad, I did not see how anything could ever come right again. Now"—he turned his gaze back to her—"I would be nowhere else."

Lisbeth thought of him as she'd first seen him, so pale, skinny as a whip, his eyes too big for his face, and that air of haunted longing about him.

Who would have thought that lad would grow into the man who lit her world? The thought shocked her even as she acknowledged the truth of it. She belonged at Rab Sinclair's side, and in his arms. Why couldn't she have seen that back then? Instead she had seen only Declan.

And now she faced the most impossible desire: wishing Declan truly gone.

****

They found Billy Dixon going over his trawler, which was still tied up at the dock, his eldest son, who sailed with him, at his side. At Rab's hail, Billy straightened and came to the rail.

"Morning, Rab, Mrs. O'Shea. Nasty blow last night, eh?"

"It was," Rab agreed. "Any damage?"

Billy scowled. He had a squat body, an unlovely face, and the habitual half-worried expression of the typical lobster fisherman.

"Nothing major. She hit the dock a few times. Soon as I go over her, we'll put out." He spat over the rail. "What's with these storms, anyway? Seems no end to them. Don't the sea gods know it's September, for pity's sake?"

"We get some of the worst storms in September," Rab replied, "when the hurricanes move up the coast."

Billy grunted. "Well, I can do without it."

"Agreed. Were you at the dance last night?"

"Me? Dance? I'm in my bed by nine o' the clock." Billy jerked his head at his son. "This young scamp was there, though, chasing after the lasses."

His son grinned sheepishly.

Rab said, "I hate to delay you putting out, Billy, but I wondered if we might ha' a word."

Billy shot a look from Rab to Lisbeth and back again. He nodded and jumped onto the dock beside him. "Something wrong?"

"Not sure, Billy," Rab replied.

Lisbeth wished she could reach for Rab's hand. Instead she tangled her fingers together and watched Billy's face.

She felt rather than heard Rab draw a breath. "When's the last time you heard from Pat O'Shea?"

"Pat?" A guarded expression came to Billy's face. "What d'you want with him?"

"His sister-in-law, here, wishes to speak wi' him." Rab nodded at Lisbeth.

"It's very important, Mr. Dixon. I think Pat may have something belonging to Declan, that I need returned."

Like his identity, she thought unhappily.

"Well, now." Billy rubbed at his stubbly chin. "Last I heard of Pat, he'd gone up to the Grand Banks. Signed on some fella's crew."

"Aye, and he's no' been back since?" The

heightening of Rab's highland accent betrayed his agitation.

"Back here? To Lobster Cove?" Again Billy glanced at Lisbeth. "No, lad. No."

"Did not stop by, maybe, to visit his friends?"

"Here now, what's this all about?" Billy no longer looked so friendly.

Lisbeth stepped forward. "Mr. Dixon, can you tell me why Pat left Lobster Cove so soon after Declan's death?"

Billy shrugged.

"But you were his closest friend," Rab pressed. "Was he in some sort of trouble?"

"Why should you think that?" Billy's expression turned sour. "He did not like staying here after losing his family—both his parents dead, and then his brother, as well. You know how close the two of them were—inseparable. Too many memories, so he said."

"But that was a year ago."

Billy spat again and looked at Lisbeth once more, pointedly this time.

"I see you've had time to move on, Mrs. O'Shea. Is Rab here your new man? A replacement for Declan, like?"

Lisbeth felt as if someone had struck her. Quite truthfully she replied, "No one could replace Declan." Except perhaps his brother, in some cruel ruse.

"I need to put out," Billy declared, "if I'm to earn any coin this day."

"Aye," Rab agreed mildly, "I need to open the forge, as well."

"Off with you then"—Billy made a shooing motion with his hands—"and stop bothering a man."

Rab smiled and nodded; he turned away and Lisbeth followed, Kelpie still glued to her side.

"I do not believe a word of it," Lisbeth said as soon as they were out of earshot.

"Nor I," Rab agreed.

"But why did he turn so ugly? And from what, besides grief, could Pat have fled?"

"We have to talk about that," Rab said seriously.

Disquiet touched Lisbeth's heart. "Tell me, Rabbie."

"That, Lisbeth, is a matter for when we're alone."

Chapter Seventeen

Rab both longed for and dreaded unburdening himself to Lisbeth about what he knew. Best over quickly, he thought as they walked home. But when they arrived, he had not one but three customers waiting, not the least a horse that had thrown a shoe.

Lisbeth and Kelpie went inside, and he stripped off his shirt, donned his leather apron, and got to work. Not until much later, when the early dark drew down, did he have a chance to catch his breath and turn his thoughts to what must be said.

How to tell someone her husband might have fathered a child on another woman? He did not know. The prospect felt even more difficult because part of him—a part of which he was not proud—wanted to destroy Lisbeth's memory of Declan. He wanted her to turn to him, instead, to see him as the better man. He needed to own up and admit that.

He entered his quarters, after closing the shop, to find the fire burning cozily and supper ready for the table. But Lisbeth looked at him with anxious eyes.

"I have your meal here," she gestured. "But if you'd rather talk—?"

"I would. Will it keep warm?"

She nodded and dried her hands on her apron. Who would have thought—Lisbeth Parsons in his home, tending his hearth. Over the years, Rab had fantasized about this a hundred times as he lay in that bed alone. And now...

He caught her hand. "Come and sit down."

"You're frightening me, Rab. Is it something dire?"

They sat facing one another on opposite ends of the bench by the fire.

"In truth, I scarcely know how to tell you. We spoke before, Lisbeth, about the things that were said of Declan."

Her fey eyes went wide with alarm. "You told me there might be proof he was unfaithful to me, but you never said what."

Sorrow on her behalf flooded Rab's heart. All at once he knew he would have wished to spare her this knowledge even if it meant she saw him, Rab, as the better man. "Lisbeth, he loved to charm women, just as he charmed you. I know for a fact one of those women was Maggie Grier at the Hogshead."

Lisbeth's skin flushed red and then drained to white. Her lips parted, but only a single word came. "When?"

"Not long before the *White Gull* came ashore. Maggie has a child—"

Lisbeth sprang to her feet and stared at Rab as if she'd never seen him before.

"His? Declan's?"

"That is what I do not know. The bairn, a wee lad, is the spit of him. I saw the child when I took Dougie home to talk to his ma about him 'prenticing. The bairn is four months old."

He saw the flicker in her eyes as she added up the months. She raised her hands to her mouth.

"But," Rab hurried to say, "it occurred to me the

child could be Pat's. You ken how alike they were. And Pat did leave in a hurry. That's why I want to talk to him."

"Billy knows something. Yes, the child could be Pat's. Pat could be playing tricks on me for some reason. But you say Declan was—was with other women also?"

"I have no proof of it. But tongues wag, and I saw him myself on more than one occasion talking to women."

"Why did you not tell me, Rab?" she wailed. "Why not come to me if you knew such a thing, and you one of my closest friends?"

"Because, as I say, I had no proof, before seeing Maggie's bairn. Because I did no' want to break your heart. And because of how I felt about you." Rab got to his feet. Helplessly, he said, "I did not want you to love him, Lisbeth. I thought if I brought you such news you might take it as an attempt to turn you from him—to me."

"By God," she breathed through her fingers, "what a tangle. I want to see her, Rab, talk to her, make her admit the truth."

"Who, Maggie? Best not."

"But only she knows whether she lay with Declan or Pat. Oh, how could he do this to me? I mean, I knew what he was—whatever you think, I am not a fool. I knew he smiled and chatted to other women. I thought it meant nothing to him; it was just Declan being *Declan*. Because he chose *me*. He married me! I thought that meant something. And I never thought he would break sacred vows."

Rab did not know what to say. He dared not touch

her, strung taut as she was. He watched tears gather in her eyes and spill over, and he thought, with sickness in the pit of his stomach, *she loves him after all.*

But it seemed these were tears of anger. "I need to see her—and this child. She knew he was married. How could she?"

Rab shook his head. "I don't think Maggie Grier lives by 'shoulds.' Pat will know the truth. I want to close the shop for a few days and go looking for him."

"He may be right here in Lobster Cove."

"So he may."

"Anyway, you can't close the shop; you need the custom."

"Nothing is more important than getting to the bottom of this." Rab ached to cradle her in his arms, but he refrained.

"How will you know where to begin looking?"

"I thought I'd hire a boat, put in at some of the ports northward, see if I can get word of him."

Slowly, Lisbeth nodded.

Giving in to irresistible temptation, Rab touched her cheek. "I want you to promise me one thing while I'm gone—nay, two things: you will keep Kelpie with you at all times, and you will stay away from that cottage up the shore."

Lisbeth nodded again and seemed to relax a bit. "I am grateful to you for telling me the truth, Rabbie. And I know you better than to think you would relate such a thing out of spite."

"Good." Rab breathed a deep sigh. He wished he could ask her for more, whether this knowledge changed the way she felt about Declan, and if, upon his return, Rab might hope for something besides friendship.

Of course for that, her husband—unfaithful or not—would in truth have to be dead.

****

Hours later Lisbeth lay in the bed alone, victim once more to thoughts that would not let her sleep. At the side of the bed lay Kelpie; she could hear her faithful guard breathing.

Too bad Declan had not proved as faithful.

She felt bruised to the point of numbness by the information Rab had imparted, but not surprised—no, not nearly as surprised as she should be. On some level had she known she did not possess all of Declan? Had she suspected that, despite the vows they took together, no one could possess all of him? Who could trap quicksilver in her hands and hope to hold onto it?

Since that first day at school when Declan held the door open for her and gave her his matchless smile, she had been able to see nothing else. The fact that Declan had chosen her above all the others who pursued him to wed—including Mignon with her fine gowns and air of privilege—had blinded her to all else.

Now she wondered what she had actually felt for Declan, besides infatuation and enchantment. Those emotions seemed so different from what she now felt for Rab: deep as the sea, strong as bedrock, vital as her own blood.

Rab had elicited from her two promises—to keep Kelpie close by and to stay away from the cottage while he was away—and she would never break any promise to this man.

Good thing, then, he hadn't made her promise to stay away from Maggie Grier.

Chapter Eighteen

Lisbeth stood near the end of Maple Street, overlooking Lobster Cove harbor. She had just watched Rab's boat sail out of sight on an achingly clear morning, all blue skies and cool air. Kelpie stood at her side, strong as a furry boulder, the dog having been instructed by his master to look after Lisbeth.

What had she seen in Rab's eyes at going? Softness toward her, longing she reciprocated. Determination, as well. They could say little to each other with Jeff O'Conner, who owned the boat Rab had hired, standing by. Jeff would sail with Rab; at least she need not worry about him sailing on his own.

A chill chased its way up her spine like the touch of winter. A year ago, a man she loved had sailed away from her and had not returned. Please God, it would not happen again.

A man she loved. And did she love Rabbie Sinclair? It suddenly seemed impossible not to love him with her every breath and every heartbeat. Only the enchantment under which she'd lived had kept her from seeing that for so long.

But now the illusion Declan had cast over her life dissipated and blew away like early mist. All the while she'd struggled to keep things together and their heads above water in the cottage up the shore, he'd been stepping out on her, seeing other women, lying to her and deceiving, coming home and trading her that smile in return for her constancy, expecting his rights in their bed. In their bed, and who else's? Lisbeth couldn't know that, but she had one name and meant to ask.

With determination she turned about, giving her back to the wide, blue sea, and started up Maple Street, the dog pacing at her side. The Hogshead would be closed at this hour. She could only hope Maggie Grier would be awake.

Lisbeth knew where the woman lived, in a tiny house out back of the tavern. She rapped on the door before which she and Kelpie waited.

Young Dougie would be off at school. Lisbeth did not want him overhearing the conversation she planned. Behind the door, though, she could hear a babe wailing. She knocked again, and an instant later the door was pulled open.

She had never before spoken to Maggie Grier, save in passing. A latecomer to Lobster Cove, Maggie had not attended school with the rest of them, though she had to be close in age to Lisbeth.

Now, Lisbeth observed, Maggie looked older. The clear light revealed lines in her face and a gulf of emptiness in her blue eyes. She wore a nightdress, not overly clean, beneath a robe that gaped open, and her blonde hair hung on her shoulders in a tangle. Behind her the unseen infant continued to cry.

Declan's child? Lisbeth's stomach clenched, and for an instant her resolve wavered. She could not do this! But she refused to continue being deceived and lied to; she wanted the truth.

Maggie looked as surprised to see Lisbeth as if she'd opened the door to receive a slap. The expression in her eyes sharpened, and a thin smile came to her lips.

"What do you want?"

"I hoped for a word. I'm Lisbeth O'Shea—"

"I know who you are," Maggie interrupted. Hostility laced her words, and her gaze swept Lisbeth head to toe and back again.

"Please," Lisbeth said stiffly. "I believe we are overdue for a conversation."

"This isn't a good time."

"Is there an appropriate time for what I need to say?"

With a grimace, Maggie swung wide the door. "Suit yourself." She nodded at Kelpie. "But leave that outside."

The interior of the little house, as small as Lisbeth's cottage, did not smell clean. Lisbeth's nose caught a hint of spoiled food, unchanged nappies, and what might be whisky, all underlain by the smell of dirt. The room into which Maggie ushered her was dim, but she could see through a doorway to another room beyond, where the baby wailed.

"What do you want?" Maggie did not invite Lisbeth to sit. Nor did she appear to notice the babe's cries.

I want to see your child, want to know if it belongs to my husband. But Lisbeth didn't quite have the courage to say the words, not faced with Maggie's hard stare.

"Don't let me keep you from picking up your baby," she said instead. "I'll wait."

Maggie shrugged. "Does him good to cry, clears his lungs out." Maggie's gaze sharpened. "Or is it him you came to see?"

Lisbeth's stomach dropped. For an instant she felt breathless.

Maggie gave another tight smile. "Who told you? That blacksmith of yours? You must be thicker than two planks if you didn't guess what was going on before this—what that husband of yours was."

"Yes, I must." Suddenly, Lisbeth's legs threatened to give way. Maggie nudged her toward a chair.

"There, sit."

She watched as Lisbeth lowered herself unsteadily, and wrapped her robe more tightly about herself. Her expression softened slightly.

"You truly didn't know? How could a woman be married to Declan O'Shea and not know? Everybody else did."

Lisbeth shook her head; humiliation burned in her cheeks.

Maggie went on, "Wasn't just me, you know. There were women all up and down the coast. He'd put out in that scow of his and go to see them—and by 'see' I do not mean *looking*."

"How often?" Lisbeth asked in a voice that didn't sound like her own. "How often did he—come to you?"

"Depended. If he was in the Hogshead drinking—mostly afternoons—he came here after. I wasn't averse; he was a good-looking man, better than my usual, if he was a bit heavy-handed in bed. I don't see the best lovers in my profession. It was all about the game with Declan anyway—not the deed. He liked charming women, winning them, persuading them to what he wanted. He thought he was...what do you call it? Irresistible."

"Did he pay you?" Lisbeth thought of how

carefully she had eked out the coin back home, how there was never enough, how they were forced to subsist most often on the little bit she earned sewing till her fingers ached. Had he taken what he did earn hauling lobsters and spent it here, not just for whisky?

But Maggie laughed. "Declan? Never! He did you a favor by tumbling you—at least that was how he saw it."

"And how did you see it?" Lisbeth raised her eyes to Maggie's face. "You knew he was married. Not even a year! Didn't that matter?"

"Why should it? If that redheaded rascal wanted to go spreading his seed around and his wife too stupid to notice, what's that to me?"

"Woman to woman—" Lisbeth began.

Maggie snorted. "What woman ever lifted a hand to help me since I got here five years ago? Which of you offered friendship? Do not come crying to me now, Mrs. O'Shea. You had his name—that's all." She lifted her chin. "I got his brat."

"Then for the love of God, go pick the child up." Lisbeth could no longer stand the sound, which had lessened to a weaker mewling.

"He'll cry himself back to sleep in a minute." But Maggie shrugged again and took herself into the other room, where the cries abruptly ceased.

She emerged a moment later with a babe on her shoulder. Even in the dim light, Lisbeth could see his hair shining like an orange beacon.

Could still be Pat's, she told herself. But Maggie had already admitted being with Declan.

Her stomach turned within her, but she said, "May I see him?"

Maggie obligingly turned the babe around in her arms. His face looked blotchy from his long cry, and he waved his fists angrily. But his eyes, which regarded Lisbeth with interest, were Declan's eyes, tawny and golden.

"Mark him, them eyes—don't they?" Maggie said with some satisfaction. "If his father was still alive I'd have no trouble making him pay for this one."

She'd have trouble getting Declan to pay for anything, Lisbeth reflected, and it shocked her that she could think of Declan with such sour acknowledgement. For so long she had determinedly kept him as her bright star. Now that image of him, like her world, had shattered around her.

"What's his name?" she asked huskily.

"Timmy. And I'll have a hell of a time raising him on my wage."

If anyone could call what Maggie did *raising*: even from here, Lisbeth could tell the child needed to be changed.

But Maggie sat herself on a second chair opposite and said, "He wants feeding, if I'm to keep him from hollering again." With no sign of modesty, she opened her robe and lowered one side of her nightgown. Timmy latched on hungrily.

"All the same, males," Maggie said acerbically. "They want the breast."

Suddenly sure she would be ill, Lisbeth gripped the arms of her chair. Her head spun in slow circles.

Declan was not the man she'd believed him to be.

Maggie gave her an appraising stare. "Ain't it about time you gave up playing the grieving widow anyway? It's been a year, and I hear you're tumbling the blacksmith."

"Where did you hear that?"

"All over the tavern that you've moved in with him."

"That's not true. I mean, I'm staying at his place, yes, but he's been sleeping elsewhere."

Maggie gave a careless shrug. "My advice, if you want it, is forget Declan. The blacksmith seems a steady sort."

Lisbeth hesitated, not knowing if she dared ask the question in her mind. At last she drew a deep breath and said, "You haven't seen him, have you?"

"Sinclair? Only when he came to ask about Dougie. Sinclair's not the sort to visit me."

"No, I meant—Declan."

Again Maggie snorted. "Not for a year. Why? Have you?"

Lisbeth got to her feet unsteadily. She knew she would see Declan every time she encountered Timmy around town as he grew. In ten years or so, would he look like the lad Lisbeth had first met at the school house that fateful day?

She asked hopefully, "You haven't seen Pat, have you? I don't suppose—well, that you were also with him?"

The side of Maggie's mouth curled. "Afraid not, Mrs. O'Shea. I've not seen Pat for an age, and anyway, he never came to call. Accept it—your man was barely your man at all. He wasn't worth your tears, so run away, little widow, and let me be."

Lisbeth did.

Chapter Nineteen

Rain slanted down in a gray curtain as Rab sailed into Lobster Cove harbor, the weather further weighing on his heavy heart. His eyes searched the harbor front for a glimpse of a big black dog and a slender woman; of course they would not be there. Lisbeth had no way of knowing when he would return.

Lisbeth. He ached for her presence as with an open wound. He wanted to touch her, yes, and claim her lips with his own, to bed her even more. Most of all, though, he just wanted to be with her, craved the warmth and safety of her company. *Home*. Lisbeth represented that to him, and always had.

It had gone hard with him, leaving her on the tail of telling her about Maggie's bairn. The news must have shattered her world. And Rab did not bring her good tidings now.

How could he expect her to put all this madness behind her and take up a life with him, Rab? For he knew his heart would be satisfied with no less.

He helped Jeff dock the boat, and they parted with no more than a nod, both anxious to get home. Rab ducked his head and ran up Maple Street, the raindrops striking his shoulders like stones. The town appeared deserted, everyone having taken cover from the rain. When he drew near the forge, he saw smoke struggling from the chimney of his quarters, and his heart leaped.

He rapped at the back door, happy to find Lisbeth had barred it. She swung the door open and bounded forth into the rain, into his arms.

For the space of several moments neither of them spoke. Rab tucked her hard against him, cuddled to his heart, and forgot about the rain.

Far too soon she lifted her face and laughed. "Come in out of the wet."

She towed him into the room, where Kelpie claimed his attention. The place felt warm and smelled of new-baked bread. The tight knot inside Rab's chest loosened for the first time within memory. He ruffled the fur on Kelpie's great head before looking at Lisbeth again.

Wordlessly, she returned to his embrace, her arms wrapping around him tight. Had she wanted this as much as he had during their long days apart? Dare he hope she might one day come to love him?

This time when she raised her face he claimed her lips with his. The kiss carried all his longing, all his need and desire. She met it with passion of her own, parted her lips beneath his even as she wound her arms about his neck. He dove into her, heedless of anything besides this craving, too long denied.

She pressed her body against his and he felt all of her—breasts, thighs, long slender legs. Her hands moved across his shoulders and tugged at his jacket.

She broke the kiss to say, "Let's get these off of you."

"What?"

"Your wet clothes."

Rab's heart thudded painfully. Did she mean all of them? He stood like an overgrown child while she

117

stripped the jacket from him and set it by the fire. Next she unbuttoned his shirt and drew that from him also. When her fingers moved to the buttons on his trousers, he caught her hands.

"Lisbeth."

It went hard with him to object. He had longed for this the whole time he was away, and stood ready for her beneath his trews. But she would want to hear what he had to say first.

She did not meet his gaze. Instead she stood quiet beneath his touch, though the collar of her dress stirred with her quickened heartbeat.

"Lisbeth," he said again, gently, "what is this?"

"Let me welcome you, Rabbie. Let me warm you." She did look at him then, raised those great, fey eyes to his, and he drew a breath at what he saw there: desire flaring bright enough to match his own.

Aye, and it would be so easy to accept what she offered, shuck the rest of his clothing, remove hers, and carry her the few steps to his bed. Worship her with his hands, his mouth—at last answer the yearning that had dogged him so long.

Make Lisbeth, in truth, his home.

He forced himself to say, "Lisbeth, I bring news."

"I don't want to hear it."

Again she pressed herself into his arms, this time making a delightful friction against the bare skin of his chest. He felt her tremble, and his desire heightened impossibly.

She tipped her head back, and her gaze once more claimed his. "I ached for this the whole time you were away, every minute."

"As did I." She must feel the weight of him

pressing against her. He let his desire for her show in his eyes, hiding nothing. Above all, his Lisbeth deserved honesty.

"Lisbeth, I would trade my soul for a night with you. But I would never want you to regret it. I think you should listen to what I have to say."

A rueful smile tugged at her lips; he felt it then— his Lisbeth had changed while he was away, had strengthened and somehow armed herself.

"Honorable to the end, Rabbie," she said with affection, "and better at guarding my welfare than I. Very well, then, tell me what you learned."

****

Again they sat at opposite ends of the bench by the fire, close enough to touch, Rab with a hot drink in his hands. Lisbeth had forced it on him along with a warm, dry shirt. Kelpie lay at his feet, as near as the big dog could get.

"I found Pat," he began without preamble. "Spoke with him, in fact. He's living in a place called Irish Cove, on Cape Breton."

Lisbeth drew a breath. Dismay flared in her eyes, but little surprise. She said nothing, though her fingers tangled together on her knee.

"He's been there since the end of the last sealing season. I do believe he means to stay. He's living with a woman he met, a widow like yourself. I spoke at length with both of them."

"That means he hasn't been back to Lobster Cove."

"It does, aye."

Rab watched the implications of that move in her eyes. She drew another deep breath, and the pulse in her throat quickened again, but not with desire this time.

"I do not suppose Pat can be behind the pranks that have been played on me, then."

Regretfully, Rab shook his head. "The woman with whom he lives—Fiona MacIvie, by name—says he's been with her since the winter. She seems an honest sort, and I believe her. She has a wee child from her first marriage and is expecting again wi' Pat's child."

Lisbeth did look surprised at that.

Softly, Rab went on, "Pat has changed from the wild lad he once was. I think he means to settle down with Fiona, for good."

"Did he say why he left Lobster Cove so suddenly after Declan's death?"

"He did not. Would not, no matter how I pressed. I do believe he was hiding something on that count. I had a chance to ask him directly when his lady went off to tend her bairn. He led me to think 'twas grief sent him off—harped on about what a great wound it was losing Declan, and the two of them so close. But I sensed something else beneath it all."

Lisbeth lifted troubled eyes to Rab's face. "What does that mean for us?"

"It means there is no easy explanation for the man you ha' been seeing. 'Tis not Pat, of that I am convinced."

"Then, who?" Lisbeth got to her feet and paced the limited space in front of fire. Almost wildly, she said, "It must be Declan. He has to be alive. He did not die at sea."

"Whisht!" Rab bade her, unwilling to have it stated aloud. The last thing he wanted, God help him, was for Declan O'Shea to be still in this world and drawing breath. He almost preferred the prospect of Declan's ghost—and what did that say of him? He knew how Lisbeth had always felt for Declan; he knew, too, just how deeply he loved this woman. Would he truly condemn her to bereavement?

Aye. Aye, and *aye*—for Declan could not love Lisbeth as much as he did. No one could.

As calmly as he could manage, he said, "I do no' see how it could be. The *White Gull* came back in pieces. How could he survive that storm?"

"I don't know either. But he was a strong swimmer; he and Pat both used to go out and flirt with the riptides."

"On a fair day, aye. Lisbeth, men who know the sea said the *White Gull* was probably struck by lightning. He'll be at the bottom of the sea."

"Then his ghost has returned, dripping sea water. I know what you're thinking—"

"You do not!"

"You think I must be mad."

"Nay, lass, for did I not see him as well, up on the coast road?" Rab frowned. It had been dark, but Kelpie had struggled with someone tangible, a flesh-and-blood man, and not Pat. Dread roiled Rab's gut and regret seized him like a sickness.

Lisbeth looked him full in the eyes. "Rab, I have a confession to make."

Chapter Twenty

Lisbeth bit her lip. Rab was not going to be pleased with what she had to tell, but she'd determined their relationship, were they to have one in the midst of all this madness, must be honest. Besides, she refused to surrender the strength she'd discovered since waking from her troubled dream.

Still holding his gaze, she began, "I went to see Maggie Grier while you were gone. I saw her child."

Consternation flared in Rab's eyes, but he sat quietly and displayed no other reaction. Declan, in similar circumstances, would have charged about and hollered, let his temper flare, cursed, and carried on.

Her heart thudded in her chest. She had to stop comparing Rab and Declan; they were nothing alike. *Thank God.*

After contemplating it for several moments, Rab nodded unhappily. "Aye, well—I should ha' known you would."

"He's Declan's child, beyond question." Suddenly restless again, Lisbeth turned away. "Poor babe." To have such a father, no less such a mother who let him lie and cry himself to sleep. What would he become?

She went on doggedly, "And that means nothing I believed was true. My marriage was not what I supposed; Declan was not who I thought. He never loved me."

The last came out in a wail Lisbeth would recall if she could. She had no right to feel sorry for herself. But she'd lived with the illusion of Declan nearly half her life, and it went hard to feel it break up around her.

"I would no' say that." The opinion came softly, in Rab's deep voice.

"Yes, well—I would. What kind of love is it that cheats and lies and deceives? I would never, never betray you so, Rab!"

She paused abruptly, all at once realizing what she had said, and the truth of it. She loved this man right down to the roots of her soul, as she had never imagined loving anyone. That, as much as the discovery of Declan's infidelity, had destroyed her dream.

Rab's eyes, blue as the deep sea, met hers without prevarication. "Nor I you, Lisbeth," he said simply. Only, she knew there was nothing simple in such a love given and received. She felt humbled, entrusted with such a priceless gift.

By heaven, she had chosen the wrong lad all those years ago in the schoolyard. And now she—now they— paid the price.

"I am sorry," she whispered.

"For what?" Rab got to his feet and pulled her gently into his arms. Warmth and comfort enfolded her, and her heart ached not with loss but longing.

"I should have known," she said into his shoulder. "I should have seen him for what he was. How could I have been so foolish, so shallow?" For she had chosen the bright waves dancing on the shore, when the deep constancy of the sea awaited her.

"Forgive me," she implored.

"There is naught to forgive." His lips traced her

hairline, graced her temple. Desire and frustration flooded her in equal measures.

"And you," she said. "You never wed anyone else."

"There never was anyone else," he answered plainly, and she felt his heart pound against her, great beats like the pulse of her world.

"Emily Cooper—"

"Emily Cooper is a fine woman. But she is no' *you*." His lips found the corner of her mouth, and she took fire like the forge when he fanned it. She wanted nothing more than to rest in this man's hands for the balance of her life, but she feared she couldn't.

She knew Rab Sinclair, guessed what his answer would be even before she bade him, "Rabbie, take me to the bed."

"Och, Lisbeth—" Resistance stiffened his muscles beneath her hands.

She reached up and trapped his face between her hands. "Will you make me beg?" She kissed him deeply, as she had never once kissed Declan. She wanted to pour her love and need into him so he could taste them. She wanted to present herself to him like a gift, without restraint. She needed to be one with him this night.

But he broke the kiss before they tumbled over the edge together, and spoke but one word. "Declan."

"I don't care." With Declan, Lisbeth had lived a lie. Rab represented truth on a level she could trust. "Ah, Rabbie, please, please!"

She emphasized the plea with little kisses on his jaw and chin.

"There is no going back from it."

"You think I want to go back? If I give myself to you this night, Rab, it's for life."

"Then I want it to be right, lass. I want you with a free heart—no strings, no ties." Very gently he put her from him and gazed into her eyes. "If Declan's alive, you are still bound to him."

She parted her lips to protest, but he forestalled her. "It does not matter if he deserves your loyalty—we know he does not. You deserve it, Lisbeth. You already lived one lie—I will no' have you live another wi' me."

She bent her head and rested it against his chest. "But I want you so."

"Aye, and I will carry that to my bed this night. But I will go. I ha' waited more than ten years for you, Lisbeth. I can wait a bit longer to make it right."

"But, Rab, how can it come right? We are no closer to answering the questions that haunt us. It would have been far better if it had been Pat playing tricks on me."

"I ken, lass."

"If Declan's alive, why hasn't he come forward and let people know? Where's he been all this time? Why appear now, and to me?"

Rab shook his head. "We will get to the bottom of it somehow, I promise."

"If he wants to see me, talk to me, perhaps let me know he's alive, maybe we should lay a trap for him. I could go back to the cottage."

"No." Rab seized her shoulders. "Absolutely not. Give me your word you won't go there alone."

"I could take Kelpie. And you could hide nearby. If we could catch him…"

"I will no' take such a chance with your safety—nor let you take such a chance."

"But, Rab, I'm no longer afraid, now I know he's alive. I will fight any way I must for what's between you and me."

"Aye, and bless you for it. But you are not going up there to lure him."

"It's just Declan."

"Is it?" For an instant, pure highland superstition shone from Rab's eyes.

"You don't believe he's alive?"

"Part of me does; part of me does no'."

"But Kelpie struggled with a flesh-and-blood person and tore his sleeve—you just said so."

Rab gave a crooked smile. "And Kelpie is named for a magical creature that can come out o' the sea or a loch and lie wi' a flesh-and-blood woman, is he not?"

"That's just a tale, a legend."

"You said yourself Declan always did have some magic about him."

He had certainly woven a spell over Lisbeth. And how many other women?

"Give me your word, Lisbeth, so at least my mind may be at rest this night."

Instead of giving him assurance, Lisbeth kissed him again, hoping to distract him from a promise she dared not give.

Chapter Twenty-One

"Is anyone to home?" The call came from the back door, which Lisbeth had left open to the fine afternoon. Yesterday's rain had flown and the clear scents of sea and wind competed with that of the bread Lisbeth had just taken from the small oven at the side of the hearth.

In the forge, Rab instructed Dougie; Lisbeth could hear the murmur of their voices punctuated by the banging of a hammer; just by listening she could tell which of them plied it.

She looked up, hoping Frannie had come to call, and instead saw Mignon leaning in the doorway.

And just where did the woman think she was bound? She wore a splendid walking suit of dark green and a matching hat that perfectly accented the color of her auburn hair. Her cheeks looked slightly flushed and her eyes bright.

"Mignon!" Lisbeth exclaimed in surprise and discarded the tea towel with which she'd lifted the hot pans. "What a surprise."

She smoothed her hands down over the plain dress she wore—one of her oldest—and rued she'd not taken more care pinning up her hair that morning. Most of it had now fallen and straggled down her neck, and her apron bore stains.

"I walked down from the bluffs," Mignon confessed. "It is such a lovely afternoon. But it is farther from the house than I thought, and now I'll need to walk home again."

"Well, sit down and take a cup of tea first," Lisbeth offered, hoping Mignon would not accept.

But Mignon agreed with alacrity. "I will not say 'no.' My, your new kitchen is cozy." She settled on the bench by the hearth and removed her hat. Lisbeth swung the kettle over the fire, wondering why Mignon had come, since they did not usually pay social calls on one another.

"I wanted to ask you to do a job of sewing for me," Mignon said, just as if she had heard the question in Lisbeth's mind. "Rather a big job, if you're not too busy now that you've moved in with Rab."

Lisbeth fetched a tea cup and the leaf ball from the cupboard. "I have not 'moved in' with him, Mignon—at least not the way I imagine you mean."

"No? Could have fooled me, with you waxing all domestic here at his hearthside. I thought you'd decided to move on, the way we discussed—after Declan."

"Not yet."

"Really?" Mignon settled more comfortably on the bench. "But it's all over town that you and Rab are a couple. Who would have thought? You and Rab! Remember how Pat and Declan used to pick on him back in school?"

"Yes, until Rab grew big enough to defend himself."

"Declan must be spinning in his watery grave. Tell me…" Mignon leaned forward conspiratorially. "How is Rab Sinclair in bed?"

Lisbeth would not readily discuss such a thing with Frannie, let alone this woman.

"I would not know, Mignon. We aren't together that way. Rab has merely acted as a friend and offered me a roof here in town—as I told you before, he sleeps elsewhere." To her dismay, Lisbeth felt her cheeks grow warm. Even lacking that intimacy, she and Rab were together on a level of which she'd not dreamed with Declan.

"Still?" Mignon looked skeptical. "Ah, well, deny it as you will, people are going to think what they like." Abruptly, she changed the subject. "How is your sister, Ellen? You know, I don't think she ever liked me."

A cat, Ellen had labeled Mignon right from the start. Lisbeth said, "She's doing well. She and her husband have a fine house in Augusta, where he practices law."

"It's odd that you didn't go and live with her, after Declan died. She could probably use your help with the children. Remind me, how many does she have?"

"Two girls. Ellen did offer to bring me to Augusta, but my home is here." Always had been, since they'd come from St. John's.

Mignon leaned toward her again, her eyes bright with malice. "So, did you want Rab even while Declan was still alive? You can tell me!"

"Of course not."

"It's all right, you wouldn't be the first woman hungry for a man who isn't her husband."

Lisbeth stiffened. "Mignon, why don't you tell me the real reason you've come?"

"Hit a sore spot, did I? As I said, I want to refurbish my wardrobe. You did such a nice job on the blue dress, I thought I'd offer the work to you rather than order out of Boston as I usually do."

Lisbeth paused in surprise. "How many dresses were you thinking?"

"Oh, I don't know—how many can you manage? Five? Ten?"

Lisbeth caught her breath. Such a commission would keep her all winter, and offer her some independence. "I'd be glad of the work," she admitted. "But I fear the gowns I produce will not be up to the latest fashion."

"Nonsense. I have pictures, and you can make them to match. Anyway, I'm looking for everyday wear in heavier fabrics for the coming season. It does get so cold up in that big house. If you agree, I'll send for the fabrics at once." She made a face. "I already checked, and Fred Beatty has nothing suitable."

"I see." Lisbeth's thoughts raced. Was there any way she could get Mignon to advance her part of the payment, something on which to live?

At that moment Kelpie came in through the back door, which remained standing open. The big dog had been lying in the sunny yard, but the smell of new-baked bread must have drawn him.

Mignon immediately tensed. "Do not let that thing in here—he's dirty and probably full of fleas."

"He's not—and he's come for a heel of bread." Mildly, Lisbeth went on, "You never liked animals, did you, even at school? I remember the time little Joey O'Rourke brought his kitten, smuggled in his pocket." Mignon had shrieked when the tiny creature got loose in the schoolroom and tried to climb into her lap.

"That cat scratched me."

"Only because you frightened it."

Mignon drew back on the bench as Kelpie passed

and only relaxed when Lisbeth distracted him with a piece of bread.

"My, how you do spoil that animal! You'll be buttering that for him next." Mignon sniffed. "Not but it smells good."

"Would you like some with your tea, Mignon?"

"I will not say no, although"—an incredible, arch look came to Mignon's face—"I really should. That's part of the reason I need a new wardrobe. That comfort eating we spoke about, before? It seems to be having a decided effect on me. I'm not the slim girl I was."

"None of us is who we were long ago."

Mignon accepted a slice of bread with her cup of tea, though she did tuck her skirts well out of Kelpie's way.

"Isn't this fun? I should walk down more often and pass the time. Maybe I can check the progress of my new wardrobe. That is, if you want the work."

"I do, but might you see your way to paying me a bit up front? It's just that I do not like taking advantage of Rab's kindness."

"Of course." Mignon's eyes gleamed. "Though I am sure you more than repay Rab in other ways—least of all by baking his bread. This is delicious." She bit into her slice again. "You know, they say new-baked bread is bad for you."

"They say a lot of things."

"Yes, and why is it what's forbidden is also what's most enjoyable? It's so much fun to live dangerously."

And, Lisbeth wondered wryly, just how much danger did Mignon encounter up in that big house of hers?

Mignon finished her bread and set her plate aside.

"Send the dog back out into the yard and fetch your measuring ribbon, Lisbeth. You will have to take all my measurements over again."

****

"Mignon was here this afternoon," Lisbeth told Rab later while they shared bowls of stew and the remains of the bread. "She wants me to make her a number of dresses—five or more."

Rab looked up and regarded her seriously. "Good news, I guess. Do you want to work for her, though? I know she sometimes puts your back up."

"So she does. But she pays handsomely, and she's the best custom in town. The work's a God's send."

Rab's big hand came across the table and covered Lisbeth's where it lay beside her plate. "You know I can provide for you, Lisbeth. I'm earning enough."

"But that's not right. You're a good and generous friend, but I need to be able to keep myself."

Rab grunted. With a hint of humor, he said, "Friend, now, am I? I'd hoped for something more."

"There's plenty more," Lisbeth returned with some heat. "You know I'd take you to that bed this instant if you'd but agree. Tell me again why we refrain, Rab. Mignon thinks we're living together in fact—no doubt the whole town does. If I have the label, might I not also have the pleasure?"

He laughed ruefully. "I am trying to spare your reputation, and your heart."

"My reputation is already accounted for." And her heart quite lost. "Mignon says a widow can do as she pleases."

"Oh, aye?"

"And it would please me to spend the night with

you." Many nights—an unbroken string of them, to eternity. She wanted to revel in the taste of his lips, the feel of his big hands all over her body, to belong to him in truth as she already did in spirit.

His fingers tightened on hers. She turned her hand within his grasp, laced her fingers through his, and pulled him toward her. Their lips met across the table and the sweetness of it exploded upon Lisbeth's senses.

"Please, Rab," she whispered against his lips.

"Ah, Lisbeth—"

She kissed him again with more heat, and heard his spoon clatter against the tabletop before his other hand came up to cradle her cheek.

"By God, lass." This time when he broke the kiss, his breath came ragged. "I love you too much to let you regret aught we may do together."

"You love me?" Lisbeth found she needed to hear it spoken again in his deep Scots burr.

"I have always loved you."

"Then, come." She got up and moved around the table. He surged to his feet also, a tangle of emotions in his eyes: desire, reluctance, and another that stole Lisbeth's breath.

She stepped up to him and began to unbutton his shirt. The soft woolen fabric fell back to reveal the broad chest hard with muscle and speckled with a pattern of black hair. She slid her palms over his skin and he stiffened like a man singed.

"Lisbeth—"

"Hush." She leaned in and let her mouth follow her hands, tasting him as she had longed to do these many days. He grasped her shoulders and the heat of his palms flowed into her.

Slowly she lifted her head and gazed into his eyes. "Touch me, Rab, as you will."

Immediately, his hands moved to her hair. He pulled out the combs that confined it; with part of her attention Lisbeth heard them hit the floor. When her hair lay in a wild mass around her shoulders, his fingers moved to the bodice of her gown, where they hesitated.

On fire for him, Lisbeth breathed, "Go ahead."

He shook his head, so she did the job for him, her fingers stumbling over the buttons in her eagerness. As she had in the stable, she shed her bodice without shame. But this time he could see her in the soft light of the lantern that stood on the table.

"By God, you're beautiful."

"I'm glad you think so."

He raised both palms and cupped her gently. Desire rushed through her like a nor'easter and settled low in her belly.

"Please," she said again, and caught his hand and drew him to the bed.

Would he, could he resist? The light came from behind him now, and she could no longer see his eyes, just the radiance washing over those big shoulders, making a halo of his black hair.

"Come to me," she bade.

Chapter Twenty-Two

Rab stood motionless as Lisbeth's hands moved to the ties on her skirt and worked their magic; the garment fell about her ankles with a billow, revealing her naked but for a pair of thin drawers—and stockings.

His heart began to pound like the hammer in the forge, and he fought to keep from reaching for her again. How many nights had he lain in that bed and longed for her, ached for just this? Ten thousand fantasies had possessed him; now the reality stood at his fingertips. How could he say no?

Yet through all those fantasies she had been another man's wife. And was still.

He could see what lay in her eyes: desire enough to warm them both, to melt away the last of his self-imposed restrictions. *His Lisbeth wanted him.* That alone made a gift that should warm him to the grave. He longed to give himself in answer, spill his need into her heat, throw himself into the sea of her desire and never surface.

But what if, when the morning came, once the flames died and the cold light streamed in, she looked at him with dismay in those beautiful eyes?

He never wanted her to regret anything they did together. He did not want the word *adultery* to rear its head between them.

"Lisbeth." He whispered it with longing.

"Touch me. Why don't you touch me?" Almost angrily she untied the laces on her drawers and he saw how she trembled. The thin fabric fell away and she stood only in her stockings—easily the most tantalizing sight Rab had ever seen.

He had imagined her so, aye, yet the truth exceeded any imaginings: breasts just full enough and now peaked in the cool air, a tiny waist, and those slender legs, skin like cream everywhere. Lisbeth, his Lisbeth.

She reached for the buttons on his trousers, a woman determined for this thing, do or die. He already stood for her, hard as an iron ingot. Once she saw the state of him, could he deny her anything?

She succeeded in her fight against the buttons and thrust her hands inside to capture him. Ah, God—he was lost!

"Lisbeth—" It seemed all he could say.

With her fingers wrapped tight around him, she looked into his eyes. "I love you, Rab Sinclair. I don't think I knew what love was, not till I realized what I felt for you. For better or worse—so it is!"

Rab's chest heaved as if he had just run up the shore. "There has never been anyone for me but you."

She stepped forward into his arms with a shocking contact of skin on skin. Rab struggled to shuck his trousers, and they tumbled onto the bed.

And oh, she made an armful—a mouthful—as he began to explore her soft warmth. Need burgeoned through him, reined only by tenderness. The flesh of her stomach felt like silk, the scent of her rose to enfold him. He had been born for this woman, had sailed the watery miles from Scotland for her, endured all the loneliness in fair exchange for this one night.

Aye, a fair exchange.

His lips skittered across her belly, made one foray downward, and returned to her breast. She fit into his mouth as if formed for it—just the right amount and no more. She sighed as he suckled her and buried her fingers in his hair. Her slender legs wove around his body, capturing him tight, and the weight of him settled very nearly where it needed to be.

An image of Declan O'Shea arose in his mind—face filled with mockery, tawny eyes full of malice.

He released Lisbeth's breast and rested his face against her, breathing raggedly.

"I canno'. We both know Declan is still alive."

"No, we don't know. Anyway, was Declan faithful to me?"

"No."

"Why should I then be faithful to him?"

She had asked this same question before. Rab had barely been able to refute it then and struggled as against a monstrous burden now.

"I want to wed you, Lisbeth." It was what he'd always wanted from the first day he beheld her outside the schoolhouse. He had decided then that she—and only she—would be his wife. He had never truly looked at another woman.

He wanted this thing done honorably, not quick and desperate.

She went still in his arms. "Oh, Rab."

"I canno' ask you to wed me, now."

"You can."

He pressed his forehead against her breast. "You are still another man's wife."

She held him tightly, and he felt her tears come. He

gathered her to him in the bed, still hopelessly hard for her, and aching. Slowly he began to kiss her tears away from her cheeks, the corners of her eyes, and her mouth.

She came to life suddenly and pressed herself against him. "Rabbie, Rabbie, if you will not complete the act—if your honorable heart will not let you—at least let me pleasure you. I know how."

She knew how. Declan had showed her, for she had certainly been with no other man. That knowledge fairly choked Rab, yet how could he refuse when her fingers once more found and cradled him, when her lips touched the skin of his chest and began moving downward? He had not wanted their first time to be like this; he had wanted to cherish her, worship her, and now there was this terrible need and her willingness, the heat of her mouth when it closed on him, and the rush so like the fire when it flared in the forge.

At the last instant he found the strength to withdraw from between her lips even as she moaned in protest, to draw her up and fuse his mouth to her breast, part her legs and put his fingers inside where she desired him. He felt the waves of pleasure wrack her, and she held to him like a drowning woman.

"Rab, Rab—" She spoke his name as he had never heard it, like a prayer. "What miracle is this?"

A year wed, and though Declan had made sure to instruct her in the other act, she did not recognize her own pleasure. What had the man been about? But nay, Rab did not want to think of Declan during this moment of intimacy—and embarrassment. For he had shamed himself after all, released his seed onto Lisbeth's soft skin even as she climaxed.

"Rab, look at me."

"Nay." He groped for his shirt, within reach of the bed, and used it to mop her flesh.

"Look at me," she insisted.

"That was not what I intended."

"Maybe not, but it was what I needed this night. Thank you for not being so cruel as to deny me."

"Lisbeth, I would deny you nothing. But you deserve better than this: honor and beauty, a lovely wedding—"

She smiled tremulously. "What a romantic heart you have, Rab Sinclair. You are not to regret this, nor be ashamed of what we share, either."

He sat up and reached for the rest of his clothes, feeling wretched and, all at once, cold.

"Stay with me, Rab," she beseeched. "Stay the rest of the night. Lie here with me."

And if he did, the same would happen again—that or more. He could not stand to be near her now without touching, tasting.

"Let me go, Lisbeth."

Her hands fell from him as if singed. She lay quietly while he climbed into his clothes, found another shirt, and told Kelpie, "Stay, lad."

At the very last he looked at Lisbeth lying in his bed, a vision from a dream.

"Be sure and lock the door behind me."

She scrambled obediently from the bed, catching up a blanket to cover her nakedness as she came. Her hair made a halo around her head as it caught the lantern light.

She seized hold of him with both hands; the blanket slid down.

"Rab—are you angry with me?"

"Nay lass, not with you."

"With yourself, then? Please do not be. This was my choice. Have I not a right to choose?"

Unable to look at her, he repeated, "Lock the door behind me."

And he went out into the dark.

Chapter Twenty-Three

"Come in; I have something to tell you." Frannie snagged Lisbeth's arm and virtually towed her into the Beckers' kitchen, out of the gray morning.

Lisbeth had something to tell Frannie, as well; it was why she had come by. If she could express to anyone her feelings for Rab and the confusion that dominated her heart, it would be to Fran.

But, as usual, cheerful madness reigned at the Becker household. Ed had already left for work—Lisbeth had seen him go—and Bess squealed in Frannie's arms, no doubt wanting to be fed. Little Eddie ran around the kitchen like the wild creature he so often resembled. Frannie, wearing a stained apron over her nightdress, did not appear to have combed her hair for days.

Despite her misery, Lisbeth smiled. Frannie might have a mad look in her eye now, but she would at some point in the future look back on these days as her happiest.

"What is it?" she asked obligingly.

But Frannie, ever the good friend beneath her distraction, looked Lisbeth in the face. "First, tell me what's amiss with you? You haven't slept."

No more had she. After Rab left, Lisbeth had struggled between anger and uncertainty. She still wanted him so much it shocked her, and she feared he

141

would not return.

Indeed, he had not put in an appearance before she left—not even to the forge. She wondered half frantically if her desire had ruined their long friendship.

What had possessed her, tossing away her modesty like that, thrusting her hands into his trousers and wrapping her fingers around him? She had never once behaved that way with Declan.

Declan. She had to discover whether she was, in truth, his widow, if only for the sake of her sanity.

"I had a bad night. Can we talk?"

"Of course." Frannie visibly thrust her own concerns aside. "I'll make tea."

She placed Bess in the highchair Ed had built when Eddie was born, now much scarred.

"Eddie, for mercy's sake go and play with your wooden soldiers. There's a good boy."

Wondrously, Eddie did. The kitchen, replete with piled dishes and sticky floor, settled into as much peace and quiet as it ever attained.

Lisbeth sat at the table. Now that she had a chance to speak, she didn't know quite what to say even though she usually shared her troubles, hopes, and dreams with Frannie. Frannie had been the first she told when Declan asked Lisbeth to marry him—or more precisely when he offered her marriage.

I'd be willing to wed you, Lisbeth, if you want. I know you, and I expect it's the only way I'll be after getting you to the bed.

She compared those words with the ones Rab had spoken last night, delivered in a voice hoarse with longing. *I want to wed you, Lisbeth.* All his heart had lain in those words, and Rab Sinclair's heart beat strong and true.

"What is it?" Frannie asked again. "What's happened?"

How much could she confide in Frannie, after all? Nothing about what had happened last night; that must stay between her and Rab. But Frannie knew so much about how things had been with Declan—the times he had worried her, failed to come home, disregarded her feelings. And all the while she had loved him.

Or had she? Had it in truth just been infatuation? For it seemed a pale shade compared to what she now felt for Rab.

She tangled her fingers together and said, "Frannie, I think I've fallen in love with Rab."

"Really?" Frannie's face lit. She sat down opposite Lisbeth, everything else forgotten. "But surely that's a good thing. You've been widowed a year; there's no reason you can't start courting."

"No."

"No? But people all over town are talking about you, anyway—best to make it official. Have you told Rab? You know, I suspect he's been a little bit in love with you a long while. And he's a fine catch. Emily Cooper's been after him like mad."

"Has she?" Just what Mignon had said, and Lisbeth didn't like the way that made her feel.

"She's always taking broken items to the blacksmith shop. I think she breaks them herself. But shouldn't you look a whole lot happier than you do, if you're in love?"

"It's complicated."

"Is it, though?" Frannie studied Lisbeth with her soft, brown eyes. "If you love him and he loves you, the way I see it you could be wed by spring."

"Aren't you forgetting something? Declan."

Frannie looked uneasy. "What about him? Oh, honey, you're not harking back to that story you told about seeing him on the shore? That was imagination, surely, and the effects of the storm."

"Was it? Frannie, I found his hat, held it in my hands."

"You've been overwrought. Happen that hat was in the cottage for months and you only just noticed it. That place wasn't healthy for you, but things are better now. And with Rab to look after you…"

"I don't need anyone to look after me," Lisbeth denied. Hadn't she been the one looking after everything during her marriage to Declan? Though the idea of surrendering herself body and soul into Rab's big hands, to his strength and care, left her breathless.

"It's time for you to snatch some happiness," Frannie declared.

"Rab and I—we quarreled last night. He went off and didn't return this morning."

"No wonder you didn't sleep. I never do if Ed and I have quarreled. I always tell him he's my peace of mind, which is a funny thing when he so often drives me to distraction. Listen to me; I've known Rab Sinclair since he arrived here in Lobster Cove. He's not the sort to stay angry or hold a grudge."

"This was no ordinary quarrel."

"So tell him you're sorry; he'll be willing to forgive."

"Maybe. But that's not why I'm here. Will you do something for me?"

"If I can."

"I want to go out to the cottage, but I don't want to go alone. Do you suppose Ed's mother would watch the children so you could go with me?"

"I don't see why not. How about this afternoon? Only it looks like rain."

The last thing Lisbeth wanted was to get caught up the shore in yet another storm. But she said, "I'd appreciate it. I promised Rab I wouldn't go alone." Or at all.

"Fine, then, I'll speak to Ed's ma and come by after lunch."

Frannie got up to pour the tea. In the corner, Eddie giggled with Kelpie. Bess sucked on her fist.

"Thanks, Frannie. Now, what's your news?"

Frannie paused and lifted the tea cup she held higher, affording Lisbeth a view of her silhouette. "See if you can guess. Only, in this loose gown, you probably can't." She set the cup in front of Lisbeth and lowered her voice. "I think I'm expecting—again."

"Oh, my! That's wonderful. But I thought you were determined to wait."

"I was. It's awfully soon after Bessie, but I swear, all that man has to do is look at me and I'm expecting." Frannie giggled, sounding like Eddie. "Well, maybe he did more than look at me."

Lisbeth glanced around the small kitchen, trying to imagine how another babe would fit. But she smiled, "Congratulations."

"I honestly don't know how I'll ever manage. But a family's always been my dream."

"I know." Lisbeth leaned her elbows on the table. "I suppose you are sure? It isn't a false alarm?"

"As sure as I can be. I have all the signs: I'm

hungry all the time, especially for sweets. I baked a cake yesterday and ate the whole thing myself. And my clothes are already getting tight. In fact, I was going to ask you to let out some of the seams if you can."

Lisbeth stared at her friend as a light suddenly flared in her mind. "Hungry for sweets?" she repeated.

Frannie laughed. "You must remember how it was with these two."

She chatted on, but for once in her life Lisbeth failed to listen.

It couldn't be. Yet, in her heart, Lisbeth knew it was: Mignon's high color, her penchant for sweet cakes, the expanded measurements for the new wardrobe... Lisbeth must have been a fool not to see.

Mignon carried someone's child.

But whose?

Chapter Twenty-Four

"Storm brewin'," Marv Chester said when he came to collect the shovel Rab had mended for him. "Big blow, if I'm not mistaken. Better get that lad home, Rab."

Rab nodded, still trying to shake the discord that had haunted him since last night. He'd deliberately come to work late so he wouldn't have to face Lisbeth over the breakfast table, or at all. She'd kept away from him all day, which he didn't take as a good sign, and had failed to come into the shop, as she sometimes did, to offer him a drink.

He'd heard her moving about his quarters late in the morning but had been busy then with Dougie, who enjoyed a day off from school. He'd not laid eyes on Lisbeth since they'd parted last night.

And he ached with her absence, as with a raw wound. Now he nodded at Marv. Sweating even though he could feel how the temperature outside dropped, he looked at Dougie and said, "Right, lad. I'll see you home."

Dougie gave him a doubtful look. "Is anything wrong, Mr. Sinclair? Have I done something?"

"Nay, lad." Rab ruffled the boy's hair with unthinking affection. "You've done well this day. But if there is a blow coming, you need to get home safe."

And he, Rab, needed to get back and speak with

Lisbeth honestly. Was he the man to be put off by a measure of embarrassment? Or by his desire for her, which now seemed to have raged into an unquenchable fire?

"Shall I come back tomorrow, Mr. Sinclair?"

"I will be that disappointed if you do not, I don't know what I'll do with myself. Now, come."

They banked the fire and left the shop, Rab resisting the need to check on Lisbeth before he went. She had been quiet all afternoon, sewing, no doubt. But Kelpie was with her, so Rab had no real cause to worry.

They went out into fitful weather, bits of spray striking them, rather than rain, beneath a lowering sky. The storm still hovered out above the sea and would no doubt come roaring up the coast all too soon.

Bent into the wind, they pushed, Rab with his arm about Dougie's shoulders to steady and guide him. They saw almost no one out and about—just the fishermen down in the harbor, hurriedly trying to secure their boats.

Rab left Dougie with his mother and turned for home, noting as he drew near that no smoke issued from the back chimney. He frowned.

Passing through the warm forge into his quarters, he found them empty. The coals of a fire smoldered in the hearth, many hours untended.

His heart began to pound. Where were Lisbeth and Kelpie? Why had he failed to check before he went out?

Like a madman, he tore open the back door and looked out as if he expected to find them in the yard. Had she been so upset with him she'd fled? Where might she go? To Frannie? He prayed so, and that she had not gone up the shore.

Heedless now of the first driving drops of rain, he hurried down the street to the Beckers', where he found Ed just arrived home and the children squalling.

Ed greeted him with a rueful smile. "What can I do for you, Rab? A bit noisy here, but step in."

"I won't, if you do no' mind. I'm looking for Lisbeth. Is she here?"

"Lisbeth? No, why?"

Frannie stepped to the door with wee Bessie in her arms. "Hello, Rab. Surely Lisbeth's back at your place by now."

"No one's there." He shook his head. "Neither she nor Kelpie."

"Well, she took Kelpie with her, but she should be long back."

Rab's heart sank. "Back from where?" As if he did not know.

Frannie looked shamefaced. "She walked up to her cottage. She asked me to go with her, but Ed's ma has toothache and couldn't watch the children. Lisbeth promised she would just go to look for something and come right back. As I say, she took the dog."

"Do you think something's happened to her like before, when she collapsed?" Ed asked. "Rab, I'll come along with you and help find her, if you like."

"No, Ed; it's going to be a big blow. Best stay here with your family."

"Oh!" Frannie reached out and seized Rab's arm. "I never should have let her go alone. Promise you'll find her."

"I will."

He ran back down Maple Street toward the harbor. Before him, the storm rushed inland, black clouds boiling above the ink-blue water. He prayed he would see Lisbeth on her way back to him, a slender figure with hair blowing in the wind. If she came to him now, he would never let her go—marriage or not.

But he saw only Ron Arnold struggling to close his shed door.

"Have you seen Lisbeth O'Shea?" Rab called to him.

Ron shook his head and hurried into his house.

At the harborside, he met the full fury of the rain. It dashed into his face like fine gravel. He called out to the nearest of the fishermen, but his voice blew away on the wind. He clambered out onto the wharf.

"Have you seen Lisbeth O'Shea?" he bellowed.

The man shook his head, and Rab made his way to the next mooring.

Not until he asked the last two men, on their way back up after securing their boats, did he get a positive response.

"Lisbeth? Saw her some time ago on her way up the shore toward her cottage. Surely she'll have sense enough to stay put there."

Rab made a helpless gesture, and the man offered, "Need us to come along?"

"No—get on home. But thanks!"

"Had that great dog o' yorn with her," the second man contributed. "Best get up there if you're goin', before the worst of this hits."

Rab nodded and pelted off, veering onto the coast track that led north along Frenchman Bay. The storm roared up the coast, and the wind, mostly behind him, seemed to lend him wings. He told himself he would find Lisbeth safe with a fire in her hearth and her door well closed against the weather.

He would tell her how he loved her and that he was willing to take her on any terms she chose. Only let her and Kelpie be safe!

****

The cottage held a deathly chill and damp when Lisbeth reached it, as if it had been empty much longer than a few days. How quickly a place lost its heart when the fire went out, she thought as she moved from room to room, looking for she knew not what.

When she came here as a bride, her dreams had been so bright. So what if the place seemed shabby, she'd thought—it was her task to make a home of it for her new husband. And how she had tried! She'd stitched pretty curtains for windows that leaked so badly for lack of putty the cold wind came in. She'd made a quilt for their bed and cooked meals out of almost nothing, for which Declan failed to show up time after time.

Now she knew why. She paused by the hearth to finger a china figurine that had been her mother's—one of the only fine things in the room. Declan must have been out chasing other women even when they first wed.

When he had come home—late—from the sea as she thought, or perhaps from the tavern, it was with a rakish, confident smile and words that rarely failed to charm her.

Don't be angry with me, darlin'—come give me a kiss, for I know you're that glad to see me.

And she had been, always, glad to see him. She'd forgiven him his failures and small lapses, as she believed a good wife should. But she didn't believe she could forgive him Timmy Grier.

She looked at Kelpie, who sat just inside the door, watching her unhappily. The dog didn't want to come into the cottage, and Lisbeth couldn't say she blamed him.

"I'll be but a moment," she promised. "We'll get back ahead of the storm."

And for what had she come looking? Proof that Declan was alive? Or dead? She needed to know one way or another if she wanted to keep her sanity, if she hoped to free herself and move on.

What would prove Declan hadn't died on the *White Gull*? One thing she knew for certain—someone had been in this cottage since she'd left. An ineffable something told her so: things had been moved, not a lot but some. She knew her home, had lived here two years, remembered how she always placed her belongings. Now it felt as if someone's fingers had been all over them. She could sense it—almost smell it.

The figurine on the mantel had been off center until she adjusted it. The dishes on the shelves of the cupboard were not as she had set them. She had left all the chairs tucked into the table and the cloth smooth; now one chair stood out and the cloth lay rumpled.

She glanced at the dog again; he returned her look uneasily.

"Has someone been here, boy? Can you tell?"

She stepped into the bedroom and her heart rose into her throat. For she could see at once someone had been lying on her bed. Like the tablecloth, she had left the cover smooth; now it looked mussed, dirty, and *wet*.

Superstitious horror traced a chill up her spine. All at once she had no doubt someone had been here in her absence. And she knew *who*.

Out in the other room, Kelpie growled. Like a woman in a dream, Lisbeth turned and walked from the bedroom, knowing already what she would see.

He filled the doorway: fisherman's boots, oilskins, and bright orange hair. "Lisbeth," he said.

"Hello, Declan."

Chapter Twenty-Five

"Lisbeth." Declan repeated her name, and she seized the back of a chair to keep from falling down. Kelpie growled again; the dog turned and backed into the room, putting himself between Lisbeth and Declan, who still stood in the doorway with the storm gathered behind him.

Back from the sea, come in storm as he had gone. Returned home. But Declan neither looked or sounded like himself.

Whatever else, Declan had always looked after his appearance. Now the red hair, long and ragged, made a wild, uncombed mop. His face appeared unnaturally pale—so pale Lisbeth could see all his freckles—and his eyes, that had always been so irresistibly full of life, looked vacant.

What became of a man who spent a year in the sea? Lisbeth shook herself mentally. That wasn't where he had been. He was no more a ghost than she was, for Kelpie could see him and clearly didn't like what he saw.

Lisbeth had rarely heard the big dog growl so much.

"What happened, Declan?" she asked softly. "Where have you been?"

"Looked for you." He waved a yellow-clad arm in a wild swipe, and Kelpie backed another step.

"Everywhere."

Lisbeth blinked. Declan had never spoken so awkwardly, not since she'd known him. Even as a lad, Declan had possessed a silver tongue that did not stumble over one-word answers. Her heart began to slam in big, painful beats.

"I was here, if you wanted to find me. Where have you been living?"

"House." This time he waved an arm behind him in the direction of the sea.

Lisbeth struggled to shrug off another wave of dark terror.

"The *White Gull* came in without you, broken in pieces."

"The *White Gull*?"

"Your boat—your trawler. Surely you remember?"

He shook his head.

"You put out to haul your traps. There was a storm."

"Storm's coming." His speech slurred as if his tongue would not quite fit in his mouth. "Lisbeth. Came home."

Lisbeth's heart twisted in her chest. Whoever this man who had come home to her after a year might be, he wasn't Declan—not her Declan with the winsome smile and the charming patter, with the lies and the excuses. His once-charming lips hung slack, and the beguiling eyes stared at her like those of a stranger.

"What's befallen you?" she asked with horror and compassion. "Was the *White Gull* hit by lightning? Did you fetch up on the rocks? Swim ashore?"

"He can't answer you; he doesn't know."

The new voice came from behind Declan. He

turned his head and moved aside like an obedient child to admit a woman who stood wrapped in a cloak against the wind. Abruptly, the rest of the pieces fit together in Lisbeth's mind.

"Mignon."

Mignon stepped in and closed the door carefully behind her.

"He's been with you," Lisbeth said, "at your house—all this time."

"Finders keepers," Mignon said with a sly smile. "That was the rule of the schoolyard, wasn't it? I found him on the rocks that night, up by my house—on that little strip of shingle. Don't you remember I showed you the path when you were there?"

"Yes."

"He didn't fetch up where the *White Gull* came in. No one thought to look so far south—no one but me. Because I was in on the plan."

"Plan? Declan—?" Lisbeth turned to him, but he merely blinked at her, his tawny eyes uncanny in the light from the lantern on the table.

"You stupid woman," Mignon sneered. "You think he wanted to be with you? Only you? Never! He was seeing me—bedding me—even before your wedding. When he went through with it, married you to spite me, so I swore—well, then I married Claude to make him jealous. And he was. He couldn't keep away."

"Not from you or Maggie Grier. She has his child."

Mignon's lips curled in satisfaction. "She's not the only one."

"I know. I should have figured it out sooner. You practically taunted me with it, didn't you?"

"You always were a stupid chit. I never understood

156

what he saw in you. But you wouldn't bed him without the ring. He got bored with you soon enough."

"So you planned to—what, steal him?"

"That's as good a way to put it as any. Once I got rid of Claude—oh, don't look so shocked, it's easy enough to do when you know what to put in a nightcap—Declan and I wanted some time together."

Declan turned his face toward her when she spoke his name, like an intelligent hound. She smiled at him—not the kind of smile she'd given Lisbeth, but one of pure love.

"He was supposed to upset the trawler in the storm that afternoon and then come to me. We figured we'd have several days and nights together before we let him be found. Just a little holiday from you, Lisbeth. But the *White Gull* got hit by lightning, and he went overboard below the bluffs."

"What—what happened to him?"

"I think he hit his head, either when he went over or on the rocks near the shore. You know what a strong swimmer he is. But even he had trouble fighting that sea in the condition I found him. I only did find him because I was watching for him, keeping a lookout on the shore. But for me, he would have died anyway. What harm to let you think yourself a widow, when you very nearly were?"

"You're mad," Lisbeth breathed.

"No, I saved him, pulled him ashore, and helped him up that path between the rocks. Like salvage, I get to keep him."

"But he barely knows who he is! Does he know who you are?"

"Oh, yes." Fondly, Mignon touched Declan's pale

cheek. "He was much worse than this at the start. Lately he's begun to remember…things."

"Me. This cottage. It's why he came searching."

"Lisbeth." Declan took a step toward her, his gaze fixed on her face.

Kelpie growled again.

"Keep that beast away from me—and him," Mignon ordered. "We'll take care of some business here, and then it will be done."

"Done? You can't expect me to keep quiet about all this!"

"You'll be very quiet, Lisbeth, before the night is through. Foolish of you, coming way out here in this weather. And how ironic for you to die in the same kind of storm as your husband. Once you're out of the way, I can reveal that Declan didn't die after all—I can have him return home. We'll have a good life together with our child and Claude's wealth. And I'll have marriage, this time, to the man I always wanted."

"Mignon—he's not Declan!"

"He is, though, deep down." Again she looked at the wild-headed creature beside her with adoration. "He remembers more of himself every day. He will forget you once you're dead. I will be his *everything*."

"You're wrong, Mignon. He knows me, he cares—else he would not have come here again and again."

Mignon laughed, a harsh, stark sound. "We shall see. Or rather, I shall. You will be at the bottom of the ocean."

"And how do you mean to accomplish that?" Lisbeth tipped up her chin. "You will never get near me, past Kelpie."

Mignon nodded at Declan. "Take care of the dog."

"No." Lisbeth stepped in front of Kelpie, who promptly butted her with his great head. "You'll not harm him."

"Then put it outside into the storm. Declan, you do it. Wouldn't want your little wife escaping now, would you?"

"Wife. Lisbeth."

Declan moved toward her, and Kelpie barked and snarled. Lisbeth buried her fingers in the fur at the back of Kelpie's neck and held on.

"Enough of this nonsense." Mignon marched to the corner and took up an oar propped there. "Finish the dog, and let's move on. We need to be done with this by the height of the storm. Then, Declan darling, you and I will wait out the worst of the weather here." She shot Lisbeth a look of pure spite. "I think I'll have him in your bed."

"Kelpie, come!" Lisbeth dashed past Declan, who stood like a rock, and hauled the door open.

"No!" Mignon screamed and swung the oar in her hands. It took Lisbeth in the shoulder and back even as the wind seized her, and Kelpie slipped from her grasp.

Behind her, Mignon shrieked, "Declan! Declan, stop her. Do not let her get away!"

Panic rose into Lisbeth's throat. She knew she must flee, yet the sight that met her eyes froze her where she stood.

The sea rose before the driving storm like a black beast and poured over the rocks toward her. She had no idea where Kelpie had gone, or which way to run.

Light spilled out the open doorway behind her. Everything else seethed with water, wind, and motion. Instinct bade her duck down against the stone break wall where she might not be easily seen. Her ears, filled by the rush of the storm, could no longer hear anyone approach. Her shoulder, where she'd been struck, screamed with agony.

Rab, her heart cried. But she could not imagine how even his love could save her now.

Chapter Twenty-Six

The storm pursued Rab as he pelted up the shore and then overtook him, roaring like a black monster. In an instant he became drenched to the skin. Far worse, he began to lose his bearings. How far ahead did the cottage lie? Could he have passed it in the dark?

No, for he thought he saw a glint of light up ahead, and then came the sound of a dog barking wildly. Kelpie? But the big Newfoundland never barked that way.

Rab gasped and, from somewhere, found the strength to increase his speed. Waves had started crashing over the rocks at his right hand. But now, blinking hard against the rain, he saw the dark bulk of the cottage dimly rimmed in light.

"Lisbeth!" he hollered. "Kelpie!"

His words were snatched away by the wind almost as soon as he voiced them. But he heard Kelpie bark again, the sound coming and going in gusts, shredded by the storm.

He ran on, the rain dashing against his back, and virtually skidded to a halt when the tableau playing out before the cottage met his eyes.

Two people stood facing one another, arguing. One of them, to his amazement and consternation, appeared to be Mignon LaMarche. The other was—

Declan O'Shea.

Rab blinked violently, but the light spilling from the open door of the cottage showed the man plainly: bare red head, stocky body, squared shoulders—it looked like Declan, but then again it didn't. Something in the stance and the way he held his head seemed wrong.

Rab could not see Kelpie anywhere, and neither of the two people standing in the spill of light saw him, Rab.

Mignon screamed, "Find her! Then finish it. Do you want to be parted from me?"

"No. Mignon, no!" Declan shouted back at her, and Rab couldn't tell to what he referred. Did they speak of Lisbeth?

"Lay the ghosts that haunt us, that haunt you, Declan! It will be better once she's gone. We'll be happy then. Free to love one another."

"No!" Declan bellowed it like a madman.

"If she tells what she knows, they'll take you away from me. Is that what you want?"

Astonishingly, Declan began to cry, the sounds barely distinguishable from the storm. For one fey instant, to Rab, Declan became the storm, raging and furious.

Kelpie chose that moment to lunge forward out of the darkness. He leaped at Declan as he had that other night on the trail, and both of them, man and dog, went down. Mignon screamed, ran to the cottage, and came back carrying what looked like an oar. She swung it high and brought it down on the struggling duo. Rab heard no sound over the wind, but only Declan struggled to his feet.

"No!" To Rab's increased horror, Lisbeth started

up from the base of the break wall where she must have been sheltering.

"Grab her!" Mignon cried, and Declan closed his arms about his wife the way strong waves might capture a boat at sea.

Rab hollered again; they did not hear him. The three of them, with Lisbeth struggling, started away toward the strip of shingle to the north of the break wall, Mignon still carrying the oar in her hands.

Like a man stunned, Rab followed. He stooped down when he reached Kelpie, terrified by what he would find. The big dog whined when Rab touched him, raised his head and licked Rab's hand. The breath left Rab's body in a rush.

"All right, boy? Can you get up?"

The dog rose to his feet and shook himself. He gazed away toward the shingle before loping off with Rab in his wake.

Madness, to go down to the shore on such a night. Waves clawed and dragged at the shingle, and the wind howled like ten banshees. Rab could barely see those ahead of him, had no hope of hearing what they said. It appeared Declan now carried Lisbeth in his arms.

What did Mignon intend to do? Toss Lisbeth into the sea? Would Declan let her? What lay between Mignon and Declan, anyway?

No time now for asking questions. He needed to get that oar away from Mignon.

He charged forward on the Newfoundland's heels and reached Mignon an instant after Kelpie leaped for her arm and knocked her down. Mignon screamed, and Rab wrestled the oar from her hands.

"What goes on here?" he shouted. "Lisbeth!"

Declan heard him this time and swung around with Lisbeth caught in his arms. The only light now was the weird radiance cast by sea and storm, but Rab needed no illumination. He had been waiting over a decade to take on Declan O'Shea.

"Put her down," he roared.

To his surprise, Declan obeyed and set Lisbeth on her feet, where she swayed perilously. Something appeared to be amiss with her left arm; it hung limp at her side.

Instinctively, Rab reached for her. "Lisbeth!"

"My wife." Declan's arm came out, barring the way. "I remember now. She is my wife. You always wanted her, Sinclair. That's why I came back for her."

Rab rarely lost his temper, but he felt rage sweep over him now, the way the sea overswept the rocks. He leaped for Declan without thought, a hundred small insults to repay and a score finally to settle.

It felt good and satisfying to smash his fist into Declan's face with all the power behind it he'd earned pounding iron. He knew Declan for a scrapper, and a dirty fighter at that, but Declan had not his size or strength. He had just hauled back for a second blow when he heard Kelpie bark again, and Lisbeth screamed.

Both he and Declan turned at the sound, their battle momentarily forgotten in mutual concern.

"Jaysus!" Declan breathed.

Mignon had grasped hold of Lisbeth and dragged her, hampered as she was by her injured arm, toward the sea. Even as Rab watched she threw Lisbeth down on the stones awash with water and lifted a rock in her hands. Her arms moved in a blur and the sea came in to snatch Lisbeth from the stones.

"No!"

Which of them bellowed it? All three—Kelpie included—leaped forward into the foam. Rab could just see Lisbeth's head bobbing in the black water, and the terrified gleam of her eyes.

Declan planted a hand in Rab's chest. "No. I'm the stronger swimmer."

He plunged into the water even as Mignon leaped in an attempt to snatch him back; her fingers missed the hem of his sou'wester by inches. With a moan, she was left standing in water to her knees.

Rab stripped off his jacket and shoes. True, he was no swimmer, but damned if he would stand by while Lisbeth—his Lisbeth—drowned in the sea. Upon the thought, he caught sight of a black blur pursuing Declan: Kelpie fought the wild water.

Rab counted the heartbeats shuddering in his chest while he strained to catch a glimpse of Lisbeth in order to swim out to her. He could no longer see any heads—light, red, or black—in the heaving sea.

Beside him, Mignon moaned again. "Gone—gone!"

"Nay." Rab saw something move in the darkness. A head—no, two. He cursed as rain drove into his eyes and he lost sight for an instant. Then...

"They're coming out," he told Mignon. "Hold on."

A crashing wave broke, soaking both Rab and the woman beside him. Out of it came the big Newfoundland, dragging Lisbeth by the back of her gown.

Mignon wailed. "No! Declan, where's Declan?"

Ignoring her, Rab dashed forward, took Lisbeth in

his arms, and towed the exhausted Newfoundland ashore. They moved all the way up to the rocks, where Rab strove for a good look at Lisbeth, sprawled across his arms.

She looked dead, but even as despair seized him she stirred, coughed, and vomited up water.

"God, Lisbeth!" Heedless, he drew her to him. "By God!"

"Declan!" Standing in the roaring foam, Mignon still shrieked and called. Rab narrowed his eyes as the sea arose in a mighty heave. In that instant, Mignon disappeared from the shore. Did the water steal her or did she plunge in, searching for the man she had chased so long?

He got to his feet and stood, striving desperately for a glimpse of either of them. None. And the fury of the storm only increased, sending waves reaching for the place where the three of them huddled together.

"Come, lad," he bade the weary Newfoundland at last, when his heart told him all hope had gone. He gathered Lisbeth up into his arms and made for the cottage, which awaited them with an open door, a single, beckoning light.

Chapter Twenty-Seven

"He returned to the sea from whence he came," Lisbeth said through chattering teeth. She could not get warm even though Rab had kindled a fire in the hearth and wrapped her in every blanket he could find. The cold seemed to come from within her, and words tumbled out, unstoppable.

"Perhaps he never was real after all."

"No, do not begin wi' all that." Rab spoke soothingly, but his voice betrayed him, as shaken as she. "'Twas a real, flesh-and-blood man I fought out there. Must I show you my hands?"

He came to sit beside her on the bench, where he pulled her into the further warmth of his arms.

Lisbeth eyed the broken skin on his knuckles and relaxed, but not much. "Are you sure Kelpie's all right?"

"Aye."

The valiant dog lay at their feet. Rab had checked him with careful fingers when they came in, taken a cloth and dried him.

"He's a hero, is this dog. Pulled you out of the sea—a thing I do not believe I could have done in that storm. 'Tis what they do, Newfoundlands. And to think Declan sneered at me when I took him in trade." Rab's voice broke abruptly and his arms tightened around Lisbeth, mindful of her shoulder. "He shall have the

167

best beef bones, one a day for the rest of his life."

Lisbeth shivered again and stole a look at the door. "What if they come back?"

"They will not, my bonny heart. I believe they are gone."

"But—"

"Whisht, lass. He was a stronger swimmer than me, sure, but he could not reach you. He tried."

"And she went after him, just as he—" Lisbeth faltered. "You're right; he was real. She kept him hidden this last year—she told me all of it before you got here. They had planned for him to scuttle the *White Gull* in that storm so they could spend some time alone together. He'd been seeing her—bedding her—since before we wed. But something went wrong. He was hurt when he ditched the trawler."

She tipped her face to look into Rab's eyes, deeply shadowed and grave. "He wasn't right in his mind, Rabbie. I don't know if you could tell."

"Aye."

"He was…empty. Not Declan anymore. But she had always wanted him so much she didn't care. She took him home with her anyway and lived with him in secret. She killed her husband so they could be together. And she let me think Declan was dead."

Rab stirred. "Pat must have known. Not that Declan had survived the storm, but that he and Mignon had cooked up this scheme between them. The *White Gull* was half his, after all. When I saw him in Irish Cove, I could tell he knew something."

"How could they all let me think him dead?"

"Mignon is—was—a cruel creature, always mean and spiteful."

"Rab, she didn't seem to care that he was damaged in his mind." Abruptly, Lisbeth's throat closed. "And she was carrying his child."

"Was she, so?"

"I almost think she wanted me to know. She came to me, asking for a new wardrobe, flaunting it. But I never dreamed, not till Frannie began speaking of her own signs and cravings. That's why Mignon decided to do away with me. She wanted to marry him herself, for the sake of the child—to bring him out of hiding as if he'd miraculously returned."

"Perhaps they were both a bit mad."

How could Mignon be otherwise? What would it be like to live with the man you adored for a year, lie with him and share every intimacy, and him little more than an empty husk?

Mignon too had dreams, Lisbeth told herself, now all awash in the sea.

The wind rattled the door, and Lisbeth started. Kelpie raised his great head and looked at her.

"Whisht," Rab said again. "'Tis but the wind, not them."

Lisbeth closed her mind to the vision of Declan and Mignon climbing, hand in hand, from the sea, white-faced and dripping.

Quietly, Rab went on, "As soon as the storm eases I will get you away out of here, back to Lobster Cove. We'll have Doc Stevens see to your shoulder, and then we'll begin anew. And you'll not come back here, ever again."

"I'm sorry I came when I promised you I wouldn't. But, Rabbie, I just had to know. We both needed the truth, if ever we could be together."

She began to weep silent, agonized tears. As he had once before, he kissed them away and whispered, "'Twill take some time, I am thinking. There is healing to be done. But I will wait for you as long as it takes, Lisbeth. Forever, if need be."

His lips found hers in a kiss of unbearable sweetness, a soft pledge given. His devotion rushed through her, dearer than warmth, stronger than comfort.

But the words would not stop flowing from her. As soon as his lips left hers, she said, "I think he must have cared for me a little. That's the reason he came looking for me, though I doubt even he knew why. He'd begun to remember, and that worried Mignon. Do you think he loved me after all?"

Rab raised his fingers and touched her cheek. "I am sure he did. Who could fail to love you? That much stayed with him, even when he came from the sea."

Lisbeth eased against his chest, releasing a small measure of pain. Kelpie, well content, sighed and lowered his head back down upon his paws.

****

The bodies came ashore three days later and were spotted by fishermen en route to their traps—first Declan's, his oilskins torn and tattered, and soon after Mignon's, her hair loose and her arms stretched out as if, even in death, she reached for him.

The news, which Rab heard down the harbor, made an answer to his prayers. He did not rejoice in the death of either of them; neither did he want Lisbeth imagining Declan making yet another return from the sea at any time. No more did he wish her to make of her late husband a martyr who had plunged to his death in a heroic attempt to save her.

Lisbeth, as he well knew, was shattered. Doc Stevens, who reset her dislocated shoulder, had spoken to him quite seriously afterward.

"Do not leave her alone. Find someone to stay with her, if you cannot."

The "someones" proved to be Frannie and, surprisingly, Emily Cooper. Ed's mother heroically took on the children during the day and Emily stayed evenings, after school.

"You will marry her, won't you?" Emily asked Rab ruefully as she left one morning. "As soon as you're able."

"Aye. I appreciate all you're doing for her, Miss Cooper."

"And I appreciate what you're doing for Dougie. But I've told you to call me 'Emily.' It's only fitting between friends."

Now, though, on this bright September afternoon, Rab had to go home and tell Lisbeth she was a widow—again. He stood for a moment above the harbor and watched a white gull take flight over the water. The pieces of the broken trawler had come home long before those of the broken man. And Mignon? She had loved too well and too constantly, like Rab himself.

He walked slowly up Maple Street to the forge. He would not give Lisbeth any of the details the men had imparted to him so eagerly: how the bodice of Mignon's gown had been torn open, or the look of terror on her face, the expression of peace on Declan's, like a child sleeping.

He hoped Declan had found peace.

The door to his quarters opened before he reached it, and Lisbeth stepped out into the sunshine. That had been happening a lot lately: she knew even before he arrived that he would come, and half the time guessed what he meant to say.

She did so now. Even as Kelpie pushed his great head against her side, she looked into Rab's face and relief flooded her.

"You've found them—ah, God!"

"Not I, lass, but they've been found, both of them. There'll be a proper burial now, and he'll haunt you no more."

"He'll haunt neither of us," she corrected. "Now do you believe, Rab Sinclair, I'm free to love you?"

"I do that, Lisbeth, lass."

"Fine, then." She tipped up her chin, and he saw the old spirit fill her eyes—those fey, dreamy, beautiful eyes that had long ago claimed his heart. "Just so you know, Rabbie Sinclair, I do not intend to wait a year for a proper marriage proposal."

Rab's world steadied around him, all the pieces falling into place. "Love, I could no' wait that long if I tried."

She tumbled forward into his arms and, at long last, Rab knew he had ended his long journey and made his way home.

**If you enjoyed *THE WHITE GULL*,
you'll want to read the sequel,
FORGED BY LOVE,
another Lobster Cove Romance
from The Wild Rose Press.
Here's an excerpt...**

Lobster Cove, Maine, August 1865

Chapter One

Douglas Grier flipped the glowing bar of orange-hot metal over on the anvil and struck it a measured blow. Sweat trickled freely down his naked back, prompted by a combination of heat and effort. The door of the forge stood open to the afternoon—bright and sunny after last night's storm—but nary a breath of breeze stirred.

He scrutinized the metal, which was destined to become part of a spar on a lobster trawler, and pumped up the fire without conscious thought. When he'd been away fighting in the south, attached to the second Maine regiment, he'd longed for just this—long days of hard work, the skill and labor of coaxing the metal to his will, the comfort of this place that so often seemed the closest he'd ever known to a real home.

Who'd think that, back at last, he would have such a hard time adjusting?

War changed a man. He'd heard that over and over again since he returned—sometimes spoken to his face in philosophical tones by men who hadn't been there, sometimes whispered and accompanied by sidelong glances. He supposed anything repeated that often must be true.

He grunted and flipped the bar again. He felt rather

1

than saw his boss, Rab Sinclair, shoot him an inquiring look. Rab frequently kept an affectionate eye on him, one of the things Douglas had missed most while he was away. But Rab, standing with his brawny arms crossed and talking to a customer, didn't pause in his conversation.

To be sure, the shop seemed uncommonly crowded this afternoon. No fewer than five customers had made their way in, and Rab's children were underfoot, as well, the two youngest ducking and playing tag as they so often did. Douglas couldn't count the times their ma had scolded them for that. And the eldest, Dorothea, sat on the top of a workbench, swinging her feet and talking for all she was worth to Douglas's former teacher, Mrs. Applegate.

Douglas stole a look at her and smiled to himself, his mood instantly improving. No one could stay gloomy in Dorothea Sinclair's company. Douglas would warrant she'd make the Devil himself grin in delight.

If Douglas had a little sister—he didn't, he had a younger brother instead, only a year or so older than Dora—he'd want her to be just like Dorothea Sinclair, bright as a brass button and twice as pretty, with black hair like her father's and her mother's dreamy eyes.

He cocked his ear now and picked up her conversation.

"I'm determined for it, Mrs. Applegate. I've been saving all my egg money, and as soon as I have enough I'll send off to Augusta for that writing course. I mean to be the very next Louisa May Alcott."

Her listener smiled. Mrs. Applegate had been called Miss Cooper before she married the new town

2

lawyer and went to having babies. She still mentored Dorothea much as Rab Sinclair had him, Douglas. In fact, it had been Mrs. Applegate who'd talked Rab into apprenticing Douglas fourteen years ago, when he was nothing but a skinny, fatherless tadpole.

Fatherless, still.

He straightened and lowered the weighted hammer to look around the familiar, dearly loved place.

The scene seemed to waver before his eyes and, as it had lately, memory intruded: a far different setting and images much less welcome.

Blood and mud, an endless sea of both. The screams of wounded horses—a sound Douglas would never forget—the cries of men strapped down beneath the surgeon's saw. The seemingly endless *boom, boom, boom* of cannon that rattled his teeth and got inside him, shook his innards till he wanted to throw up.

He'd been fortunate, though, he told himself firmly. *Fortunate.* The Union Army had been quick to make use of his skill at the forge, attaching him to an encampment just behind their lines. He didn't have to wear the blue uniform that strained over his burly shoulders—at least not all the time—nor carry the rifle with its deadly bayonet, which had surely been invented by the Devil himself.

He had been called upon to use his skills for a variety of causes, from mending caissons on the fly to cauterizing the stumps of severed limbs. There had even been that one time…

He drew a breath that expanded his broad chest, remembering, and the forge disappeared before his eyes. Instead he saw a dark night and a white moon, sharp and cruel as a sickle, flying before a hot wind.

Douglas had been roused from his weary bed by his friend Donner, who worked supply for their outfit and had his fingers in a host of pies.

"Shh!" Donner cautioned him at once. "Don't wake anybody up."

That had been enough to make Douglas swallow the curse that hovered on his lips. Only half dressed, he rose from the narrow cot and followed Donner out into the gusty darkness.

"Fetch your pincers, hammer, or whatever else you'll need to break iron," Donner whispered. "I got a job for you."

The Army had fitted out a mobile forge for Douglas that could move along with their lines. He ducked inside and snatched the required tools without looking. "What—?" he began.

"Shush," Donner said again. "Nobody can know."

Without further explanation, Donner led him off through a cornfield, half of which had been burned in the wake of the retreating Confederate army. Nearly a year before the end of the war this had been, somewhere in southern Virginia. Douglas remembered the scent of the stalks surrounding him as he struggled to push through them in the wake of the much smaller Donner. On the far side of the field stood a copse of trees, and there, close beneath their shelter, had gathered a group of people—two Union soldiers, neither of whom Douglas recognized, and five Negroes huddled close together as if they shared one heart.

Startled, he shot a look at Donner. They had strict orders to steer clear of the local populace, brown or white, and not involve themselves in what their corporal called "politics."

4

"You're here to fight." *Maim, mutilate, and slaughter people*. Right, and what had that to do with politics?

"What—" he began again.

In a low voice, Donner replied. "They're on the run. We're helping them."

"Escaping?" Douglas could not tell which appalled him more, the idea that one man might honestly suppose he owned another or being dragged from his cot to become enmeshed in such a situation.

No one said anything, and Douglas tumbled to the foolishness of his question. What else would they be doing out here behind the northern lines in the middle of the night?

One of the Union soldiers spoke after a lengthy pause. To his further surprise, Douglas caught the glint of sergeant's stripes on his sleeve.

"Their plantation burned, about five miles west of here—house, slave quarters, and all. They made it away in the confusion. Crosby, here, is going to smuggle them back further behind the lines and away."

Douglas nodded, realizing not all the stench of burning came from the field.

"Men after us," said one of the Negroes, his voice deep as the night. "Don't have much time."

Douglas eyed the group of two men and three women. In the light from the moon their faces had a similarity born of expression, all stoic caution. The man who had spoken had grizzled hair, and the second, who looked younger, might have been his son. One woman, clearly elderly, wore a kerchief knotted around her head and leaned on a stick; the other two appeared much younger.

5

"They're chained up," Donner explained. "Need you to break them apart."

Chained?

The older man raised fisted hands, and Douglas saw it for truth. Emotion tore through him; he didn't lose his temper often, but it wasn't every day he saw people constrained like livestock.

He gave a hard nod and gestured the fellow forward to a boulder that lay at the edge of the field. "I'll be glad to."

The man moved, and the others came with him. Only then did Douglas see they were not only shackled but chained to one another, as well.

Grimly, choking back hard on his outrage, he set to work. All dignity, the old fellow bent and laid his hands across the rock; Douglas carefully placed his chisel and raised the hammer to force the hasp. The sharp sound of breaking metal seemed to echo through the night.

The younger man shouldered the first aside eagerly and set his clenched fists on the rock. Moving quickly now, Douglas transferred his anger into force that made short work of the man's shackles, which the fellow then kicked aside before he helped one of the younger women to his place.

When she bent down, Douglas saw she was heavy with child. She, in turn, assisted the old woman; Douglas worked gently on those fetters and moved them away carefully when they came off.

The last of the women quickly stooped to hunker at his feet. She stretched her hands eagerly across the cold rock, and Douglas glanced up to encounter her face, lit by the moonlight.

She was beautiful. Young and willowy, with a

smooth brow, prominent cheekbones, and a tapered chin, she had hair that crinkled all around her face and great, wide eyes even darker than Douglas's own. For an instant their gazes connected, and it felt just as if someone punched Douglas in the heart. Surely he could glimpse her soul in those eyes—twice as beautiful as her face.

"Hurry," Donner bade.

She had delicate wrists and slender, clenched fingers that made the shackles seem an even greater abomination. With all his heart, Douglas wanted the cruel, dirty, rusted metal away from her skin. He accomplished the task with a series of sharp blows, and when the chains fell away, she grasped his hands.

"Thank you. Thank you, sir!"

And what a voice she had! Deep for a woman's, and soft as velvet. Douglas stood like a man struck—or stupid—while she scrambled up and, with a lingering look for him, joined her companions.

Donner laid a hand on Douglas's shoulder. "Best night's work you ever did, I'll bet."

Douglas nodded, giving it but half his attention and too busy regretting the loss of the young woman's touch.

The sergeant gathered his little flock. The other soldier snatched up the broken shackles and chains. A hot wind stirred the branches, and a cloud moved across the moon, sending flickering light into Douglas's eyes. Yet he saw how she looked back at him still, her gaze once more reaching for his.

Laughter in the forge brought him back to himself and the scene—one he had already relived a hundred times—disappeared from his mind's eye.

7

He had no regrets about the task he'd performed that night, save one: he should have asked her name. Why had he failed to ask her name so he might hold it in his heart?

Following are a few brief excerpts from other Lobster Cove books and stories from The Wild Rose Press, Inc.

Her mother had been nearly incoherent with distress. Was something going on she wasn't aware of? She was seventy-one now. Maybe looking after a rambunctious five-year-old was too much for her.

No. Dr. Campbell was the one who was wrong.

"I know my mother. She didn't do this. It was an accident."

"We'll soon find out. Sharon is questioning Ava now."

"She'll be scared, all by herself."

"Sharon's very good at what she does. She has a way of making kids feel comfortable."

Julia turned on him, the anger and despair she'd been holding inside spilling out. "And you? Do you enjoy upsetting five-year-olds and turning families' lives upside down? Does it make you feel powerful to sic the authorities on us?"

"Look, Mrs. Stewart, I take no pleasure in bringing in the authorities. But I've seen child abuse, up close and personal, and I can tell you it's damn ugly. The things parents and caregivers are capable of doing to defenseless children…"

He stopped abruptly, his chest heaving. Closing his eyes, he averted his face and took a deep breath. When he turned back to her, his steely control was back in place. "So, yeah, if I have even the smallest suspicion that a child has been abused, I'm going to ask questions. And I'm not going to apologize for it."

THE WIDOWS' GALLERY

Abigail Adams Longley looked around at the three women flanking her in Hall 10/14 of the Uffizi Gallery. They were all staring at *The Birth of Venus* like wide-eyed art students. Admittedly, the painting was as compelling as when the Medici family originally commissioned the tempera on canvas in the fifteenth century. But for Abigail, seeing the painting again wasn't cathartic. It was beautiful, but that wasn't the feeling she was going for. Peace. Why couldn't she get some goddamned peace in this life?

Abigail glanced at the square-cut, four-carat diamond on her finger, gazed at the sparkle of the ring she hadn't removed since the day Louis had proposed. And now, a whole year after his death, she still hadn't taken it off. Conventional wisdom dictated that you weren't supposed to make any major life decisions until a year after a spouse's death. Well, it had been a year already, and she hadn't wanted to make even one decision—major or minor—about where to live, where to go, or what to do. Whoever said money can't buy happiness had devised another dead-on axiom. She had all the money in the world—in fact Louis had left her a big chunk of the globe. He'd left her set for life, monetarily. But she would have traded every cent for the chance to be with him again. Louis was gone, and the sooner she faced the fact that she was alone on this planet, the better off she'd be.

SOMEDAY MY PRINTS WILL COME
a short fantasy

"Mr. Emissary, just for the purposes of discussion, if ever we became lovers—that is to say, if I were yours and you were mine, and I held your heart—would you honestly want me to seek variety, as you call it, with other men?"

He hadn't considered that. It was a trick question, and he thought it best to answer it with silence.

"That's what I thought. I've heard it told that fidelity can be quite a turn-on. In my opinion, it is a virtue. You should keep that in mind."

She had cleared away the plates, and they were sitting on a very roomy and comfortable couch in front of a roaring fire, looking out the window at the waves crashing, drinking wine that tasted like the nectar of the gods out of crystal goblets, and munching on delicate slices of those almond cookies Eva was always baking.

"What do you put in these things?" He thought it was very definitely some kind of a love potion, because he was feeling more amorous by the moment.

"Calm down. I told you before, they're just cookies." She drew a breath and continued. "I've been thinking, and after some consideration, I've decided to let you instruct me in the ways of seduction."

He choked on his wine and had to put the goblet down. He was speechless. The things that came out of her mouth were a constant surprise.

"I'm beginning to like the sound of this," he said eagerly, moving closer to her. "It's not every day a man gets to initiate a goddess. I imagine there would be a lot of pent-up demand, over the centuries."

"I'm talking about love, Mr. Emissary, not sex."

A word about the author of *The White Gull*...

Born and raised in Western New York, Laura Strickland has been an avid reader and writer since childhood. Embracing her mother's heritage, she pursued a lifelong interest in Celtic lore, legend, and music, all reflected in her writing. Author of Scottish romances *Devil Black* and *His Wicked Highland Ways*, she has also penned The Guardians of Sherwood trilogy, two Buffalo Steampunk Adventures (*Dead Handsome* and *Off Kilter*), and the holiday novellas *The Tenth Suitor* and *Mrs. Claus and the Viking Ship*. For Valentine's Day 2016 she has written *Ask Me*, part of The Wild Rose Press's Candy Hearts series.

She can usually be found at home near Lake Ontario with her husband and her "fur" child, a rescue dog.